The Final Season

Planet Gallywood #1

Andrew Gillsmith

Mar Thoma Publishing

Copyright © 2023 Andrew Gill Smith

All rights reserved

The characters and events portrayed in this book are fictitious. Any similarity to real persons, living or dead, is coincidental and not intended by the author.

No part of this book may be reproduced, or stored in a retrieval system, or transmitted in any form or by any means, electronic, mechanical, photocopying, recording, or otherwise, without express written permission of the publisher.

ISBN-13: 979-8367783919

Cover design by: Rafael Andres
Library of Congress Control Number: 2018675309
Printed in the United States of America

Dedicated to my wife Cheryl, who has brought purpose, meaning, and joy to my life.

CONTENTS

Title Page
Copyright
Dedication
Characters
Prologue ... 1
Chapter 1 ... 8
Chapter 2 ... 14
Chapter 3 ... 20
Chapter 4 ... 29
Chapter 5 ... 35
Chapter 6 ... 41
Chapter 7 ... 49
Chapter 8 ... 54
Chapter 9 ... 60
Chapter 10 ... 67
Chapter 11 ... 74
Chapter 12 ... 80
Chapter 13 ... 86
Chapter 14 ... 92
Chapter 15 ... 99

Chapter 16	104
Chapter 17	111
Chapter 18	117
Chapter 19	121
Chapter 20	126
Chapter 21	130
Chapter 22	138
Chapter 23	143
Chapter 24	149
Chapter 25	158
Epilogue	162
Acknowledgements	167
About The Author	169
Books By This Author	171

CHARACTERS

The Rexans

Galfos Tfliximop (an ancient scientist of repute)
Gumpilos Tfliximop (his descendant)
Cniphia Obgulagong Tfliximop (Gumpilos' wife)
Gusto - aka Gus (their son)
Pnethius Bentarik (an anarchist leader)
The Prime Minister

Gallywood types

Betty Neezquaff (Chief Showrunner)
Elvie Renfro (Junior Writer)
Rufus Camford (CEO of the Network)
Edwina Mummington (Neezquaff's aide)
Mr. Kratsch (A shadowy villain)

PROLOGUE

If the inhabitants of Rexos-4 had anything resembling a common creed, it would almost certainly have been "Mxtlpicam' bnak ooligapn," which in most languages translated to something like "What's the bloody point?"

In the original Rexan tongue, the question mark had long ago been dropped; deemed as not only unnecessary but also contrary to the spirit of the expression. There was indeed no bloody point, and the Rexans damn well knew it.

Nevertheless, the galaxy-wide broadcast of their day-to-day foibles and misadventures–now translated into over two hundred million languages with closed captioning–preserved the unnecessary diacritical symbol. Many suspected that this was strictly for merchandising purposes. *What's the Bloody Point?* had been the most popular entertainment franchise in the known universe for over 10,000 years. Billions upon billions of mobile communication devices offered the expression as a catchy ringtone, prompting titters of delight and polite chuckles from the outer rim all the way to the core of the galaxy. Alarm clocks awakened the bleary-eyed denizens of a thousand star systems with the question each morning, usually delivered with the deadpan nasal hilarity most associated with Rexan culture. On the insouciant planet of Yorf, the most popular toy was an adorable-looking stuffed animal that could be programmed to respond "What's the bloody point?" whenever Yorfan parents asked children to tidy their rooms, do their homework, or perform any other number of tiresome chores.

Whatever the motivation, phrasing it as a question had proven to be a monumentally good business decision.

It is important here to note two key facts: First, the Rexans had no idea that they had been entertaining the rest of the galaxy for ten millennia, preoccupied as they were with the inevitable, and now imminent, destruction of their planet. Second, it was not always thus.

On the contrary, the Rexans had once been a rather irritatingly industrious people, full of vim and vigor, constantly inventing things and devising new theories on the nature of the cosmos. When ancestors of the audience of *What's the Bloody Point?* were capable of little more than bludgeoning each other to death with stones or waggling half-evolved flippers that still lacked opposable digits, the Rexans had already built telescopes that could peer deep into the recesses of space and time.

Needless to say, they took to the secrets of electromagnetism like ducks to water, and within a relatively short time, Rexos-4 was radiating signals out into what the Rexans believed was a mostly empty and terribly dull void.

Things changed–and not for the better so far as the Rexans were concerned–when one of their astronomers by the name of Galfos Tfliximop, performed a series of astonishingly complex calculations on the orbital dynamics of a nearby three-star system. After spending several months on the math, Galfos finally arrived at a solution in the middle of the night. Upon finishing his work, he got up from his desk, poured himself a glass of blorkin milk, and wrote a brief note to his sleeping wife before hanging himself by the neck in his garage. In true Tfliximop family tradition, Galfos was far better with numbers than words. The note simply read, "Mxtlpicam' bnak ooligapn," without a question mark.

It was not until weeks later, when Mrs. Tfliximop delivered Galfos's company-issued computer to her husband's erstwhile employer, that the reason for his fatal existential crisis was discovered. One of the stars in the nearby system was destined to break free of its unnatural celestial ménage and collide with the dusky middle-aged sun that held Rexos-4 in orbit. Like a spurned lover, this rampaging ball of superheated hydrogen and helium would leave a swath of destruction in its wake, incinerating most of the Rexan solar system and breaking up what had been an unremarkable, but nevertheless stable, relationship between Rexos-4 and its own life-supporting star.

In other words, the Rexans were doomed.

Now, to be fair, every living thing in the universe is doomed. In fact, some species scarcely have an opportunity to relax, stretch their legs, and ponder questions of metaphysics and ontology over a cup of tea before cruel death takes them. The typical lifespan of the quintz flies of Oberon, for instance, is just thirty-seven seconds, despite an average IQ somewhere north of 400. As a result, their civilization has never really gotten off the ground. The greatest quintz fly accomplishment was the discovery of the Fibonacci sequence, which an individual fly once managed after just twelve seconds of sentience. Sadly, this da Vinci of the species was unable to pass on the new knowledge to future generations, having been eaten by a quintz frog in the thirteenth second of his life.

Even the interdimensional Ubrakians, who loved nothing more than to lord their so-called "immortality" over everyone else, would eventually succumb to the heat death of the multiverse, ruled as it seems to be by catastrophe, chaos, and entropy.

This basic predicament, known by all and yet rarely voiced in polite company, was perhaps the reason for the broad and enduring appeal of *What's the Bloody Point?* It spoke to what the dominant species of one minor planet called "the human condition," a term they had coined because they were humans. More ecumenically, it spoke to the condition of all sentient life, a rich pageant of sorrow, joy, love, longing, tragedy, transcendence, and complaints about the weather, all punctuated not with a question mark but with a final, dreadful period. In this respect, the Rexans were no different from anyone else in the galaxy. And yet entertainment being what it is, the show somehow allowed sentient life forms to forget this bothersome aspect of reality precisely by focusing on it so intently and so specifically. It helped that production values also happened to be quite high.

Even the poor quintz flies eventually found a way to tune in, though of course they were never able to finish a full season and were constantly asking one another things like "Who is that character?" or "Why are the Rexans all so morose?" before they died.

Elvie Renfro, an uncommonly pious member of her species who had recently been hired as a junior writer for *What's the Bloody Point?*, firmly believed that God, too, watched the program and perhaps even enjoyed it. For, as a poet from her planet's distant past had once said, "Eternity is in love with the works of time."[1]

Still, fans of the Rexans rightly pointed out that it was one thing to know that one would eventually die–that in fact all life and all traces of it would finally disappear–quite another to know the exact method, manner, and date of one's own demise.

This, the Rexans of old had calculated down to the nanosecond.

After Mrs. Tfliximop had deposited her dead husband's computer with the receptionist, a bored and (if one were being honest) rather nosy IT worker had perused its contents hoping to find something interesting, along the lines of a private sex tape or a saved draft of an email exposing the company's senior management for crimes of capital imbecility. Instead, he found a file labelled, disappointingly, "The End of the World." The mathematics therein were so far beyond his comprehension that he had nearly wiped the hard drive clean then and there out of sheer spite. But as fate would have it, he decided that it would be safer to report the finding to Mr. Tfiximop's manager.

Government agents showed up at the poor IT worker's apartment complex a few days later, questioning him about the contents of the hard drive and whether he had discussed them with anyone else. It would no doubt have been quite distressing, but for the fact that all memories of the hard drive, the interrogation, and everything else that had happened since last Tuesday were obliterated from his mind by an injection administered by one of the agents at the conclusion of the meeting.

Sadly, no power in the universe has been found that can contain calamitous news, and word soon began to trickle out about "The End of the World" file. It got so bad that the prime minister of the Rexan parliament went on television to give what he'd hoped would be a reassuring fireside chat.

"My dear fellow Rexans," he began. "Many of you have heard the specious rumors and conspiracy theories concerning the so-called end of the world, which is alleged to occur in approximately 15,000 years, seven months, forty-four days, and nine hours and fourteen minutes. This is, of course, preposterous…"

And then, most unexpectedly, it hit him: the bleak tableau of certain annihilation. The erasure of every achievement of the people of Rexos-4. The end of history, as it were. And so he stuttered his way to a full stop on live TV. Yes, the apocalypse was a still a good ways off, but dash it, it was coming and there wasn't a damned thing they could do about it.

What followed next has now been downloaded over 17 quintillion times, making it one of the most viewed clips in the history of media. The prime minister, a lifelong politician and expert liar, sat in front of the cameras and told the unvarnished truth to the people of Rexos-4. Scientists throughout the galaxy have confirmed that a stranger, more improbable event is unlikely ever to occur. Shortly thereafter, he suffered a vote of no-confidence and was said to have retired peacefully to the countryside, where he spent the remainder of his days bouncing grandchildren upon his knees and painting mediocre landscapes in watercolor.

So began Rexan society's precipitous decline.

It is ever the industrious idealists who suffer most when their illusions are shattered, and the agony of Rexos-4 in those first few centuries was no exception. What had once been a prosperous and conscientious society that lacked even the words to describe such concepts as "smoke break," "afternoon nap," or "brunch" devolved quickly into...well, into what it is now. That is to say, a planet full of malcontented layabouts who have raised laziness, apathy, and all around chapfallenness into a literal art form. A planet whose unofficial creed is "Mxtlpicam' bnak ooligapn."

The universe is a big place, and it all might have amounted to a proverbial fart in the wind were it not for the discovery, by pure chance, of Rexan's faint electromagnetic signals by the unlikeliest and most unworthy of creatures– a writer. Almost overnight, the writer's career prospects were transformed. He had spent the past ten years unsuccessfully pitching publishers on a 900,000-word grimdark, steampunk, enemies-to-lovers romance, paying his bills by writing pseudonymous erotica involving sentient (and horny) Calabi-Yau manifolds. But now...now he was producing works of such sublime pathos and surpassing poignancy that he shot straight to the top of the heap. Like any self-respecting writer, he declined to disclose the true source of his newfound inspiration, which he had stumbled across one evening while fiddling about with an old ham radio that had once belonged to his father.

The writer would have gotten away with it, too, and lived out the rest of his days as a celebrated and sensitive soul whose art had blossomed late in life had not one of his natural predators–a literary critic–not stumbled across the exact same broadcast from Rexos-4. The critic promptly exposed the fraud, which had the predictable effect of increasing the writer's sales.

Others picked up the broadcasts as well, and before long a large entertainment conglomerate purchased the universal rights to the content in perpetuity. The first few episodes were panned by critics, but the tale of the tape was in the audience numbers which, to put it mildly, were astronomical. It was a hit.

Even hit shows cannot go on forever and *What's the Bloody Point?* was no exception. In fact, this was to be its final season, for the rogue star was even now tumbling towards the outer planets of Rexos-4's system, its gravitational presence disturbing them like egg-swollen hens at the unexpected approach of a farmer.

As such, ratings had never been higher, and the showrunners were feeling the worst kind of pressure that these unhappy creatures can possibly experience–the pressure to bring ten millennia of undiminished success to a satisfying conclusion.

If you happen to be one of those gentle souls blessed enough not to work in the entertainment business, you may be blissfully unaware of just how dire the situation was. Bringing a show, any show really, to a satisfying conclusion is one of the most difficult problems in the universe. Certain mathematicians, when asked how it could be done, have opted instead to devote their entire lives to solving unproven, nine dimensional theorems that would give even quintz flies sudden heartburn. There are microbes huddled on the condensed, frozen cores of gas giants beneath the crushing weight of tens of thousands of miles of radon atmosphere who console each other with occasional reminders that, for all their troubles, they at least aren't expected to satisfy fans and critics watching for the slightest misstep at the end of a good series. On more than a thousand planets, theologians have offered as evidence of God's mercy the fact that He did not, in fact, require His only-begotten Son to work in a writer's room during a final season.

I offer these feeble comparisons in the hope that they might in some way explain certain regrettable decisions that were made by the producers of *What's the Bloody Point?*, decisions that will be discussed not only in the coming pages, but surely until the last Ubrakian turns out the lights and the curtain falls upon all life.

CHAPTER 1

From a very early age, Gumpilos Tfliximop sensed that he was not like other children. The signs were many and varied. He nearly always completed his schoolwork on time. He ate his vegetables before dessert. He occasionally even tidied his room without being asked. But the biggest difference was something harder to measure and altogether more alarming, a certain peculiarity of his interior life that, if he was not careful, constantly threatened to break free of all discipline and express itself, naked and raw, to aghast onlookers. He was an optimist.

On the planet Rexos-4, nearly all lifestyles were tolerated, save one. In any town of modest size, one might find nudists, self-flagellating agoraphobes, religious fundamentalists, punspeakers, or even people who preferred microwaved popcorn to stove-popped. What one did not find were optimists.

Optimism had all but vanished from Rexos-4 millennia before, when one of Gumpilos's ancestors had calculated that the planet would be obliterated by a rogue star on a quite specific date in the then-distant future. That date was now a mere nine months away.

As Gumpilos grew from an awkward, redheaded stripling with a lazy third eye into a slightly less awkward adult, he learned to keep his rosier proclivities to himself. These days, he almost never said louche and disreputable things like "I'm sure it will all work out in the end," or "The sky is always darkest just before the dawn," or "How can you know unless you ask her out?"

This evolving maturity suited his parents just fine. In fact, it did more than that. It relieved them of much anxiety. They had worried about the boy's future throughout his childhood, wondering at times if such a seemingly blinkered lad would even survive long enough to experience the apocalypse that was scheduled to occur on his twenty-seventh birthday.

Gumpilos loved them very much, so much that the strain of concealing his true nature seemed a small price to pay for their peace of mind. The Tfliximops were an ancient and respectable family, after all. Some thirty members the clan had committed suicide in the spirit of "Mxtlpicam' bnak ooligapn" over the years, nearly twice as many as their patrician rivals the J'knotlovs. It wouldn't do at all to spoil the family name so close to the finish line.

The larger problem, so far as Gumpilos was concerned, was that he differed from his family in another way. Unlike most Tfliximops, he was not a gifted mathematician. In fact, he preferred poetry, of all things, to calculus. Were it not for the fact that eccentricity was practically *de rigueur* among the Rexan upper class, this might have had unfortunate consequences for his career prospects.

No, Gumpilos was not gifted in any discernible way except one–everyone seemed to like him. Not in a garrulous, back-slapping, "next round's on me" sort of way, for it has already been noted that he was a bit awkward. Rather, Gumpilos provoked in others a deeply-felt, subconscious pity that moved them to want to help him. This arrangement might, in some corners of the galaxy, constitute proof of the existence of God, for Gumpilos always did seem to need help. His father, ever on the lookout for the best interests of his only son, therefore encouraged him towards a career in sales.

And so it was that, despite his nagging anxiety that he had failed to live up to his illustrious forbears, Gumpilos Tfliximop managed to carve out a relatively pleasant if unfulfilling existence by the age of twenty-six. He had his own house in a gentrifying neighborhood that still bore a few traces of its hipper, more Bohemian heritage. He owned several pieces of original artwork and a genuine leather sofa. He even had a modest investment portfolio, though the stock market had really been shite for the past hundred years or so on account of the impending end of all life on Rexos-4.

The thing he did not have–and never had–was a girlfriend. That, however, was to change on a certain fateful morning.

****

Cniphia Obgulagong was a journeyman barista for the largest coffee chain on Rexos-4. The name of the outfit had changed several times over the years, reflecting the sadly deteriorating state of Rexan culture. Originally, it had been called Morning Delight. Later, the shareholders relaunched it as Innervating Liquids and later still as Why Not Some Hot Caffeine? At present, it was called Please Hurry, There is a Rather Long Queue After All.

There was always a queue at Please Hurry. The Rexans of course did not mind this one bit, for queueing was something of a planetary pastime. To them, life itself was in some sense merely a queue unto death.

The job suited Cniphia perfectly, for she was both unapproachably beautiful and resolutely misanthropic. Corporate valued the latter quality greatly, and so they would send her from store to store as a roving paragon of the ideal Please Hurry employee in the hopes that some of her habits might pass, almost via osmosis, into her co-workers.

On this particular morning, Cniphia was in a particularly foul mood. Several of the stores employees were late for work, a common enough occurrence, but she had also forgotten her favorite flair button, the one that read "It's coffee, not rocket surgery...make up your bloody mind already." To make matters worse, the tip jar was dry as a salt pan.

Her mood did not improve when the customer in front of Gumpilos, who was standing in the same line, changed his mind at the last minute and decided that he did not, in fact, want steamed blorkin milk in his latte.

"Right," said Gumpilos rather more cheerfully than he intended, for as we have stated Cniphia possessed the kind of remote beauty that on other planets tended to inspire epic poetry or profuse sweating from the upper lip.

"Right, what?"

Gumpilos was startled, but he answered with his usual reflexive pleasantness. "Nothing…just, you know, 'right' as in, 'hullo,' or 'umm…' or 'good morning.' It's filler."

"You seem the sort of chap who might order a decaffeinated beverage," said Cniphia with unnecessary honesty and observational keenness.

It was true that Gumpilos frequently took iced herbal teas rather than the amphetaminic draughts preferred by most Rexans to start their days. But he was feeling rather more adventurous (and dare I say optimistic) than usual this morning. Something stirred deep inside of his soul, something primal and undomesticated, very nearly alien. This rough beast, which Gumpilos had not, until that very moment, even known lived inside him, stood up, stretched its legs, and whispered to his ego, saying "For heaven's sake, do try not to say anything that would make you sound more of a twat than you already are." He so desperately wanted to impress her.

"As a matter of fact, I will have a quattro shot of piping hot espresso, m'lady. *Sans* blorkin milk." The beast inside Gumpilos groaned silently, shook its head, and went back to sleep while several customers in the queue behind him suffered quiet attacks of sympathetic embarrassment.

Cniphia merely grunted, rang him up, then jerked her head slightly to indicate that he should step aside until his order was ready. Gumpilos did as was expected while entertaining the fantasy that the pretty barista was flirting with him.

His reverie was interrupted a minute or so later by

Cniphia's barking, accompanied by some unkind titters from the queue.

"Oi, you, the lanky redheaded tosser with the lazy third eye–your coffee's ready!"

I do not know, dear reader, if you believe in fate or destiny or true love. Opinions on these matters vary considerably, and it is not for me to foist my own beliefs upon you. So I will say only this. First, until that precise moment in time, Cniphia Obgulagong most assuredly did not adhere to such romantic notions. And second, it doesn't really matter what one believes because the events that followed collapsed a quantum wave function and made it impossible for any outcome to happen other than the one that actually did happen.

Gumpilos was so startled that this latter-day Helen of Troy was speaking to him, that he had completely forgotten what it was that he had ordered. He shuffled forward as if in a trance, all three of his eyes fixed upon Cniphia's radiant face, picked up the hot espresso drink from the counter, and proceeded to chug it down as if it were a flacon of mountain dew collected by winged faeries and served over ice.

As was often the case in such situations, Gumpilos' body had registered his error in judgment before his mind, causing him to spew the espresso out of his mouth like the eruption of a small, dirty volcano on a low gravity moon.

The misty ejecta hit Cniphia square in the face a few milliseconds later at a high rate of knots. Gumpilos, desperately seeking anything that would soothe the nuclear burns he was sure were inside his mouth, grabbed the nearest room-temperature object he could find, which happened to be a bouquet of day-old cake pops that were being offered at half price. These, he stuffed into his mouth, despite wondering if they would melt into pudding and burn his gastrointestinal tract.

A stunned and pregnant silence descended upon the store.

For a moment, it was as if time itself stood still and that

the fate of the entire universe was balanced upon a razor's edge. Most eyewitnesses would have taken odds of a hundred to one on Cniphia tossing poor Gumpilos out of the store, along with the banderole of cake pop sticks that protruded from his mouth like a roll of ammunition for a Tommy gun.

Instead, the corners of her mouth began to twitch slightly upward like a pair of squirrels racing one another hesitantly up a tree. Forthwith, her shoulders and stomach trembled, and she raised a tentative hand, initially to wipe some espresso from her forehead but, at the last possible second, to cover her mouth instead. When the laughter finally broke free, it was with the force of a long-dammed river rushing over rocks and furrows remembered fondly from its youth.

Gumpilos stared at her, suspended somewhere between rapture and relief, not knowing what to say, and unable to speak on account of the encumbrance of cake pops.

Cniphia, having tamed her guffaws to a mere giggle, spoke first.

"I get off at 5:30pm. You should take me out for dinner."

"Certainly!" Gumpilos spluttered, extracting the charred bundle of sticks from his mouth. Then, with his innate optimism getting the better of him, he dared to press his good fortune. "But if it's not too much trouble, might I have an iced ickleberry tea to go?"

CHAPTER 2

Now, wait just a minute, you're probably thinking, isn't this plotline all a bit too on-the-nose? I mean, you're telling me that a descendent of Galfos Tfliximop–the man who in a very real sense launched the entire franchise–is now conveniently falling in love on the eve of the very apocalypse his ancestor had predicted? And on top of all that, you say that his name is Gumpilos? Puh-lease.

To this, I can only say that reality is often stranger than fiction. And also that it is considered impolite to pass judgment on the naming conventions of species outside one's own.

Besides, nearly everyone in the universe falls in love at some point, whether there happens to be an impending apocalypse or not. The ways of the heart exist beyond time and reason.

To say that Betty Neezquaff did not find these arguments convincing would be an understatement. She had built a well-earned reputation as an inveterate hard-ass on a number of shows before being brought in to guide *What's the Bloody Point?* to a soft landing in its final season. During her tenure as executive producer of *Ice Barbarian Surf Club,* the trade press went so far as to dub her "Body Count Betty." Lest you think that a compliment, *Ice Barbarian Surf Club* was a prime-time sitcom. Many believed her to be the perfect person to oversee the final season of the program, for like all members of her particular mafia, she excelled at the unsentimental subversion of all tropes.

And so she had done the obvious thing by striding into

the writers' room that morning to knock some sense into the pitiable denizens who toiled there.

She had just finished a particularly withering critique of the treacly, and worse, thoroughly un-subversive romantic subplot involving Tfliximop when, to her astonishment, she heard a high-pitched, yet kitschy, voice that could best be described as the sonic equivalent of a baby numbat dressed in pink footie pajamas skipping through a rain of glitter whilst carrying a parasol.

"Ms. Neezquaff," the irritating voice interrupted. "It's just that, well, this *is* reality programming after all…"

Neezquaff's head swiveled about the room scanning for the source of this Tinker Bell insolence.

So sweet and innocent was this utterance that Neezquaff had half-expected to find it coming from one of those baby cherubs you see in old paintings. Instead, it appeared to be emanating from the mouth of a rather unattractive, ill-kempt young woman whose spectacles and mousy mop of hair lacked any discernible style, and whose asymmetrical face was punctuated by a large mole on her forehead. The dissonance was jarring, even to a grizzled veteran like Neezquaff. And so she said the first thing that came to her head.

"My God, girl! You look like you've just lost a ferocious boxing match — Your face resembles nothing so much as a rear view of Orion's low-hanging bollocks."

(Reader, here I must remind you that I merely report what had happened. This does not imply that I condone it. Ms. Neezquaff's remark was not only uncharitable, it was also a gross exaggeration. It is true that Elvie Renfro was not attractive by the standards of her species or any other, but she was hardly so grotesque as to deserve the aforementioned insult. It would be fair to describe her as "plain," or even "homely." But she was not some Medusa, likely to turn any soul unfortunate enough to meet her gaze into stone. I might further add that Neezquaff herself was not a candidate for Miss Galaxy. She had, over the years, been pumped full of such quantities of silicone and plastic that it off-gassed continuously from her pores, lowering the sperm count in any room she entered. Her platinum hair was swept up into a taut bun, making it look if her face had been stretched over her skull and cinched in the back.)

If Neezquaff had hoped to unnerve the girl with her verbal assault, she was sorely misguided. For Elvie Renfro happened to be imperturbable. Insults and profanities that would shock the leaders of biker gangs on Grishnak-9, or send seasoned stand-up comedians scurrying offstage in tears, simply washed over her with no discernible effect. There are two possible explanations for this, and in the interest of fairness, I think you should have both. The first is that it was an adaptation of sorts. A defense mechanism. All her life, Elvie had been blessed with the voice of an angel and a face resembling that of a deep-sea creature hauled up by a trawler. She had therefore become accustomed to insults and provocations, and had learned early on that the best course was to ignore them rather than to engage. The second explanation is simply that she was created this way, with a nature as sweet as her voice was and a face that wasn't. It wouldn't stretch the imagination to assume that she had been designed by a higher power who had endowed her with a superabundance of kindness, gumption, and equanimity in order to serve the interests of some hidden, happy destiny.

Anyway, Betty Neezquaff's stare having found its target, was a planet-destroying death ray, causing the other writers to press back in their seats as if experiencing lethal g-forces. Elvie simply met the mogul's eyes with an infuriating look of nonplussed innocence.

"Oh do go on, Ms.…I'm sorry, I didn't get your name."

"Renfro, ma'am. I'm Elvie Renfro, the new hire."

"Continue, please, Ms. Renfro. I'm quite eager to hear your thoughts." Neezquaff intensified her death stare, but it simply passed through the junior writer as if she were a prismatic nebula, refracting and splitting into beams of pure menace that hit everyone in the room but her.

"What I mean to say is, should we really be tampering with the storylines at all? Our audience expects *What's the Bloody Point?* to be unscripted, natural. I like to think of us not so much as writers but as humble gardeners who pluck the juiciest berries from the orchard that is Rexos-4 and serve them up to the delight of our viewers."

It was then that Neezquaff smiled. Nobody could possibly be this naive, not in the entertainment business. This saccharine little creature must surely be a practical joke of some kind, planted by one of her rivals or perhaps even a critic from the trades.

"Is that so, Ms. Renfro?" she indulged, determined now not only to play the game to its end, but to emerge victorious.

"Quite so," said Elvie.

Neezquaff folded her arms and paced the room. "It may surprise you then to learn that the producers of this program have frequently intervened in the affairs of Rexos-4 in service of plot, pacing, and general character development. In fact, one might go so far as to say that everything that has happened on that unhappy planet for the last ten millennia has been scripted."

The producer, sensing that her rhetoric had achieved the desired effect, stopped pacing and put hands to hips. The little naïf kept a brave face, but Neezquaff had made a career out of ending careers and could literally smell the saline deliciousness of tears forming inside the ducts of the girl's eyes. I do mean "literally," for Betty Neezquaff's species had evolved as ruthless predators in the ancient biosphere of her home planet. As a consequence, her olfactory sense was remarkably advanced.

Sensing that victory was at hand, Neezquaff pressed her case.

"As you know, we have cloaked drones all over the place to record various happenings, plots, and subplots. But you are perhaps unaware that we also have an army of plants who have helped guide the narrative."

"Plants?" said Evie plaintively.

"Not the green growing kind, you imbecile. I mean we have our own people on the ground, whispering in ears, pulling on strings and generally ensuring that the show doesn't bore everyone to tears! Did you really think our sponsors would fund something so simultaneously prosaic and helter-skelter as an unscripted reality program?"

Evie chewed on her lip, trying to think of what to say; a futile pursuit as Neezquaff had no intention of letting her speak.

"The planet wouldn't even exist were it not for our interventions! We have saved Rexos-4 from certain destruction no fewer than a dozen times during the run. Just one-hundred and fourteen seasons ago, the Visikoshians had to alter the local laws of physics in order to evaporate a bowling-ball sized black hole that had drifted too close to Rexos-4. I can assure you that this was as tedious as it was obscenely expensive. And do you think that the Rexans could have come up with a vaccine against the Great Plague of 27439 on their own? Please! This is to say nothing of the various wars, rebellions, and natural catastrophes we have prevented. Few things that happen on Rexos-4 are accidental or natural!"

Neezquaff paused to soak in her triumph, inhaling the scent of Evie's disenchantment as if it were perfume.

"But…but…"

"Spit it out, girl! I don't have all day to listen to you blubber."

"But…that would mean we could save them if we wanted to."

"Save them? What do you mean?"

"You just said that we have prevented a dozen apocalypses on Rexan-4 over the last ten thousand years. Couldn't we prevent this one, too?"

Neezquaff's laugh was like a gamma ray burst from a star collapsing in on itself, a place from which nothing–not even hope–could escape.

"It is one thing to fix faulty plate tectonics or give some hapless researcher the genetic code of the Tleilax virus or evaporate a small black hole, you stupid cow. But there is no way to stop a giant red star careening out of control. Not even the Visikoshians could manage that!"

"But couldn't we evacuate them?"

This suggestion, if one may call it that, was so jarring, so improbable, so utterly against Neezquaff's storytelling ethos that she was now absolutely certain that she was being trifled with. All that remained was to discover the identity of the unseen puppeteer pulling on the strings of the horse-faced marionette who was presently wasting her valuable time.

"You think we should evacuate them?"

"Well, yes," replied the girl whose skin looked as if it had been tenderized to prepare a tartare.

A low growl rumbled in Neezquaff's throat. "Do you have any idea how trite that would be? Ten thousand years of buildup and then poof! We whisk them all away on magic chariots. That would be the trope to end all tropes. I can scarcely conceive of a greater offense against modern narrative science! The critics would hunt us down and kill us, and what's more we'd deserve it. This conversation is over. Everyone get back to work!"

And with that, Betty Neezquaff turned on her heels and exited the writers' room, wondering why she didn't feel the buzz of victory coursing through her veins.

Such insolence will not go unpunished, she thought as she jabbed the up button in the elevator lobby. She had every intention of firing Elvie Renfro the moment she got back to her top-floor office.

CHAPTER 3

Gumpilos had a harder time concentrating at work that day than usual, preoccupied as he was with the prospect of his coming date with the beautiful barista whose name he had neglected to ask amidst all the morning's excitement. Still, he made several sales to clients who found him irresistibly charming, if a bit dim. Each of them, after agreeing to the purchase, felt as if they had done something rather noble or charitable, along the lines of rescuing a lost duckling wandering in traffic or donating to an orphanage.

The hands of the clock towards quitting time proceeded at an unbearably glacial pace, which struck Gumpilos as odd given how time had appeared to be rushing forward so quickly these last few years. Everyone on Rexos-4 seemed to be in a perpetual hurry, whether they were checking things off of bucket lists, experimenting with new drugs, or simply stocking up on toilet paper in advance of the apocalypse.

When five o'clock finally came around, it was as if the singing of angels had burst forth from the heavens.

Gumpilos quickly tidied his desk before throwing on his coat and locking the office door behind him. Never before in the history of short walks had a short walk seemed longer than the one that took Gumpilos from his office to the Please Hurry down the street. He arrived ten minutes early and lingered outside so as not to appear as eager as he evidently was. I am sure I do not need to remind any of you of the dangers of such idle time. Doubt and fear cruelly tormented him, and he began to wonder if his exquisite encounter had all been a dream. It is entirely possible that someone less optimistic than this late-generation Tfliximop might have succumbed.

Nevertheless, Gumpilos knuckled up some courage and strode through the door of the coffee shop at precisely 5:30pm.

His sudden appearance at closing time had both startled and annoyed Cniphia, who in truth had forgotten that she had asked him out on a date.

"Oh, right. You," she said by way of pleasantries.

"Gumpilos Tfliximop at your service," said Gumpilos with a slight bow and a sort of curlicue flourish of his hand gesture that that began at his forehead and ended in deeply felt embarrassment. "I don't think I actually ever caught your name!"

Cniphia rolled her eyes, silently cursing both herself and her mother, whom she blamed for her present predicament, among a great many other things.

"I'll be back out in a minute. Just have to lock up the stockroom."

I would be lying if I told you that Cniphia hadn't considered sneaking out through the back door. But then she realized that her date was exactly the sort of fat-headed galoot who would remain standing there until the morning, at which time she would have to endure him once more. *Best get this over with*, she thought.

So, instead, she steeled herself for what she was certain would be one of the most unstimulating nights of her life.

Back in the lobby, she found Gumpilos looking over the bags of coffee beans and branded merchandise as if he were a discerning collector in an antique shop, as she knew he would be.

"Ready?" he asked, rushing to open the door for Cniphia on the way out. This compounded the air of awkwardness because the door was heavier than it appeared to be, forcing Gumpilos to lean in with all four hands.

"There is a good noodle shop just down the way," said

Cniphia, not exactly lying. The noodles were indeed good, but the reason she chose the restaurant was because it was known for its lightning-fast service. She figured the ill-conceived date could end in about an hour, unless there was a queue.

"Capital!" said Gumpilos, prompting a chuckle from his date.

"Do you always talk like that?" she asked.

"Like what?"

"Like someone has shoved a probe up your bum all the way into your head, and the probe has discovered that the contents of your cranium are completely empty."

"Hmmm," said Gumpilos. "No one has ever asked me that before! I can't say that I know. I just talk the way I talk, I suppose."

As everyone knows, awkward silences are commonplace on first dates. They are in fact the *sine qua non* of first dates. This silence between Gumpilos and Cniphia, as they made their way to the noodle shop, however, was longer, more silent, and more awkward than most. I daresay both were mightily relieved when they finally arrived at the restaurant.

Gumpilos, who was raised to be a gentleman, held the door for Cniphia and then positioned her chair for her once they were shown their table.

I should say here that Rexans take their noodles seriously. There are over four thousand known shapes, and it was commonly believed by nearly every inhabitant of the planet that that you can tell a lot about an individual Rexan by his or her preferred dish. It was in essence a substitute astrology, though far more interesting, for rather than being restricted to a mere ten or twelve constellation-based signs, noodle-ologists had an almost limitless palette with which to work their auguries, especially when one considered the variety of sauces involved. Noodle shops were therefore akin to temples on Rexos-4, the scene of not only a plenitude of first dates, but also anniversaries, birthdays, going-away parties, end-of-life celebrations, job interviews, breakups, and business negotiations. They were often rather fraught with auguries and portents.

Now, as a matter of personal belief, I don't hold with astrology of any kind. I don't object to it on moral grounds, per se, but rather on a more general principle of vanity. I should like to think that I am a completely unique individual rather than a mere "type" and I extend to my fellow sentient creatures a similar courtesy. Still, even I must confess that Rexan noodle-ology was often vexingly accurate.

Cniphia, for instance, ordered a bowl of zza-zza, which were a rough-textured, lightning-bolt-shaped, gluten-free confection. It might not surprise you to learn that she also ordered one of the spicier sauces on the menu.

Gumpilos did himself a disservice by ordering a Mlongk-Blongk sauce over bowties. Mlongk-Blongk, more an insipid gruel than a sauce, is quite popular with accountants, residents of nursing homes, and copy editors. In Gumpilos's defense, he would ordinarily have gone for a more respectable fish sauce, but the epithelial cells of his mouth and throat were still smarting from the morning's espresso incident.

Another issue with divination, whether it is based on the stars or on pasta, is that it lacks any kind of real rigor. In the case of Cniphia and Gumpilos, for instance, one could find compatibility charts warning that a match of such divergent personalities could never possibly work out just as readily as one could find charts cooing vapidly about how "opposites attract."

Fortunately, neither of our subjects read too much into the other's order. Cniphia because she had already made up her mind that Gumpilos was an excruciating prat and Gumpilos because he, on account of his latent optimistic tendencies, nearly always chose to see the best in other people.

Having placed their orders, they were now obligated, by the ancient and universal laws governing such affairs, to engage in conversation. Cniphia, who had already sussed out her date as the sort of blighter that one could wind up and allow to talk for hours, asked Gumpilos an open-ended question. I do not rightly know if this tactic is based on instinct or if it is something that females of most species must learn, but no one can argue with its efficacy in a wide range of dating situations.

"So," she said. "Tell me about your family."

"Ah...yes! The Tfliximop clan," replied Gumpilos. "Where to begin? Well, given present circumstances–by which I mean the supposedly impending end of all life on our fair planet–I suppose I could begin with my ancestor Galfos. He was the one who first discovered the star that will presently incinerate us and calculated the date down to the microsecond."

"Wait–did you say your last name was Tfliximop?" Cniphia exclaimed, her interest now mildly piqued. By mildly, I mean to say that she was no longer casting furtive glances from her third eye towards the kitchen wondering when their waiter would emerge with their noodles. All three of her exquisitely beautiful eyes were now fixed on Gumpilos. "I saw a documentary about you lot on the RBC just last week!"

"Yes. *The Harbingers of Doom*, I believe it is called. They're airing it rather a lot these days" said Gumpilos rubbing all four of his strangely muggy palms on his pants. The documentary was a bit of a sore subject for him.

"You weren't in it," said Cniphia.

This statement of fact related to the reason why it was a sore subject. As I said earlier, in addition to his unseemly optimism, Gumpilos suffered from chronic but generally manageable anxiety about his status, vis-à-vis the more illustrious members of his family. He had originally been quite excited about the movie covering the great generational span of Tfliximopos only to have his hopes dashed when the director told him that not only would he not be in it, but that it would be decent of him to avoid the family's ancestral home entirely while they were shooting.

It is said by the wise that in order to display courage, one must first feel fear. As pertains to Gumpilos Tfliximop, one could never be certain if it he was being brave or simply displaying a lack of situational awareness. For my part, I like to believe that he often knew exactly what he was doing and should therefore be celebrated as one of the great heroes in the history of gumption.

"I'm afraid I'm a bit of a disappointment. I…I didn't merit inclusion."

By now, Cniphia had entirely forgotten about their order, which was taking a suspiciously long time to arrive. This was something new for her: a boy who was not bending over backwards to impress her on a first date. What's more, he wasn't affecting a lack of interest or a devil-may-care facade. He was simply being honest. For the first time in her life, Cniphia felt that she had perhaps been too quick to dismiss Mlongk-Blongk sauce tipped over bowtie pasta. and its partisans.

"What do you mean by that?" she asked. "The bit about not meriting inclusion—" Another open-ended question, though this time she was genuinely interested in the answer.

"I mean that in the long and illustrious line of Tfliximops, I am a bit of an oddity. A disappointment, one might say."

"You're not a celebrated mathematician, then?"

"Oh, goodness, no. I'm in sales."

Cniphia snorted, thinking at first that Gumpilos was pulling her tail, for she suffered under the same delusion as many others that success in sales required a high degree of extroversion, self-confidence, and articulateness.

"Oh–you're actually serious?"

"Quite!"

"What do you sell?"

"Time capsules."

Cniphia, while far from being as unguarded as Gumpilos, was not an especially suspicious person. And yet, once again, she was sure she was being bamboozled.

"Time capsules? You sell time capsules to people on a planet that is set to be cremated by an alien sun in less than eight months?"

"Oh, I can see why you might be confused!" said

Gumpilos, waving his quartet of hands. "They're not those kind of time capsules, the kind you bury in the ground. We sell time capsules that can be launched into space! They're shielded against radiation, surrounded by a temporal bubble, and guaranteed to last at least one million years, with certain provisos of course."

"Provisos?"

"Yes–I mean, we can't be held responsible if they fall into a black hole, or if you tried to sneak antimatter batteries onboard or somesuch. The usual."

"And what do people put in these time capsules?" asked Cniphia.

"Anything and everything, really. Photographs, mix tapes, flowers, currency, mummified pets…you name it! I must say, business has been in fine fettle recently."

"I'm sure it has," said Cniphia, a bit crestfallen. The imminent apocalypse was every bit as sore a subject for her as the documentary was for Gumpilos. Suddenly, she remembered something he had said at the beginning of the conversation, back when she thought he was an insipid prat.

"Wait…what did you say earlier about the apocalypse? I believe you described it as 'the supposedly impending end of all life.' Am I to understand that you don't believe it will happen? That it's all some kind of a hoax?" Despite her hardboiled exterior, Cniphia felt a faint stirring of hope deep in her belly, directly adjacent to the spot that was now beginning to rumble with hunger.

"Oh not at all. I'm quite certain it will happen…in this unfortunate timeline."

"What is that supposed to mean?"

"Well, another one of my ancestors had a theory, a sort of alternative to the standard mish mosh concerning quantum mechanics and the collapse of the wave function and whatnot. It's all quite over my head of course, but the gist of it is that there are an infinite number of universes, each one representing a state of possibility. I find that metaphor helps me get my bean around it. If you think of reality as a kind of giant tree, with branches constantly splitting off in various directions based on decisions, events, and–oh, what's the expression—"

"Quantum observations?"

"Bob's your uncle! That's the very phrase I was looking for. Anyway, he called it the Many Worlds Theory. I think it's a jolly way of looking at things, though of course there is no way to know if it is true or just a load of tosh."

Gumpilos had no way of knowing it yet, but Cniphia was one of those large-brained girls given to periodic bouts of melancholy. She was seized with one such flare-up forthwith.

"So according to this theory, there's a world where, for instance, our dinner has already arrived and we already on dessert?" she offered.

"Rather!"

"And one where the restaurant is closed on account of a kitchen fire and we have to go elsewhere?"

"Deffo!"

"And one where I called in sick and we never met this morning?"

Gumpilos had not considered this particular scenario, but he couldn't fault the logic.

"I suppose so."

"Hmmm..." said Cniphia. She did not verbalize her melancholic thoughts, namely that under this Many World Theory, there was a alternative reality where her parents were not dead, that she had enjoyed a happy childhood, and that the world was not set to end in a matter of months.

"Ah! Our noodles arrive," said Gumpilos, who had already affixed a napkin to his shirt collar like a bib and was rubbing his ensemble of hands together in glee.

The two ate in silence, though the content of their quietude could not have been more different because Gumpilos was focused entirely on his food while Cniphia's mind was racing across this newly-discovered multiverse like a honeybee in a field of wildflowers.

From time to time, she looked up from her bowl of zza-zza and met the eyes of her date, eyes that were, she now noticed, the kindest and most honest she had ever seen. Guileless, in fact. And then something else began to stir in her, a different kind of hunger.

When they had both finished their plates, Cniphia wiped her mouth delicately with a napkin and proceeded to ask a most indelicate question.

"You're a virgin, aren't you?"

The waiter, who had appeared at precisely that moment to deliver the bill, snickered and shook his head knowingly. On Rexos-4, as on every other known planet, waitstaff were among the most astute observers of human nature, tips being a great inducement to the cultivation of this skill. He had figured Gumpilos a virgin the moment the couple walked through the door.

Gumpilos blushed the color of the Rexan sun.

"I say! Well…er…"

"What do you say we remedy that this very evening? My flat is just around the corner."

Gumpilos found the suggestion agreeable, not out of base lust, which was inimical to his nature, but because he had already fallen quite in love.

"I say that would be tickety-boo!"

Later that night, after several rounds of intimacy, Cniphia fell asleep with her head resting on Gumpilos's shoulder, and Gumpilos smiled up at the ceiling, thinking that of all possible worlds, this one was perhaps the very best.

CHAPTER 4

A more impulsive executive might have fired the troll-faced little ingenue on the spot, but Betty Neezquaff did not rise to the top of the entertainment industry by acting upon impulse.

No, in order to reach such lofty heights, one had to possess a Machiavellian shrewdness along with the sang-froid of parents of Piligastian triplets and an ego the size of a small moon. Even more so if, like frau Neezquaff, one was not blessed with a raw storytelling talent.

So it was that she began the process of dotting i's and crossing t's immediately after slamming the door to her office.

"Edwina!" she shouted through the door to her administrative assistant, whose teeth were still rattling from the force of the aforementioned door-slamming. "Bring me the personnel file on Evie Renfro, the new writer!"

"Straight away, Ms. N," came the reply.

Moments later, Neezquaff nearly jumped out of her skin when her assistant appeared phantasmagorically in front of her holding the file. Edwina had this ethereal way of entering rooms without anyone noticing. This was no doubt on account of her species being able to teleport across short distances. It took some getting used to, given that she had only been on Neezquaff's team for a few weeks, following on from the sixteenth assistant to have been given their marching orders.

Neezquaff sprang from her desk to snatch the file, licking her cruelty-thinned lips in anticipation. With luck, there would be no booby-traps in the girl's background, and that she could be terminated with extreme prejudice within the hour. Edwina, in the meantime, had vanished, presumably back to her desk in the reception area.

"Yes, yes…hmm…right. Excellent!" said Neezquaff to herself as she reviewed Elvie's curriculum vitae. There was nothing remarkable about it. No red flags. Nothing to suggest that she was un-fireable. On the contrary, she had all the markings of one of the legions of tyros whose careers in Gallywood were roughly equivalent to the lifespan of a quintz fly.

Without looking up from the dossier, Neezquaff once again summoned her assistant, in *magna voce*.

No sooner had she relaxed her tonsils than Edwina was once again standing before her, smiling officiously.

"Yes, ma'am?"

"I want you to have that gruesome mole rat of a writer sent up here at once. I intend to fire her in the old style."

"I'm afraid she's already at lunch, ma'am," said Edwina. The woman had a near-clairvoyant knowledge of what was happening at all levels in the organization, which made her simultaneously indispensable and detestable.

Thinking to toy with her assistant a bit, Neezquaff asked, "Oh, is that so? And what is she having for lunch? Spare no details! I must know which condiments she prefers!"

"I can't say that I know the answer to your last question, ma'am," replied Edwina again with that cheekily punctilious expression on her mug. "You'd have to ask her uncle, with whom she is presently dining in the employee cafeteria."

This seemed a rare bit of good fortune, almost too good to be true. If she hurried, Neezquaff would be able fire the girl in front of her uncle as well as hundreds of employees! Such a move would only add to her fearsome mystique.

"Then I shall go to her!" she cackled. "The employee cafeteria on the twenty-third floor, you said?"

"The very same. You will find her in an alcove booth with

Mr. Camford." The corners of Edwina's permanently pursed lips betrayed what generous souls might describe as the hint of a smile.

Neezquaff froze in her tracks, like a lonely ice-fisherman who had just heard a loud crack in the vicinity of his fishing hole.

"I'm sorry," she said, one eye beginning to twitch involuntarily. "I thought you said Mr. Camford—"

"That is because I did, ma'am."

"Pray tell, why would a lowly, bulbous-nosed proboscis monkey of a writer be having lunch with the president and CEO of the network?"

"Apparently, she is his most cherished niece, ma'am. If that is all?"

Neezquaff nodded queasily and sat back down at her desk to collect her thoughts as Edwina teleported herself back into the reception area.

So that explains it, then. Nepotism! I should have known!

Indeed, she should have known, for nepotism was both traditional and widespread in the entertainment industry.

Still, thought Neezquaff, *there may be a way to turn this to my advantage.*

"Edwina!" she shrieked once again. "Call the elevator and hold it for me."

"Of course, ma'am."

"And press floor twenty-three while you're at it. I'm heading down to the cafeteria after all."

****

Neezquaff's entry into the cafeteria was akin to a shark gliding over a reef at dusk. A ripple of fear preceded her as little clownfish retreated into protective anemones, crabs burrowed into the sand, and cephalopods desperately tried to camouflage themselves against their surroundings. This, Neezquaff had anticipated, for it was the customary response whenever she entered most rooms.

The sudden hush made it all the easier for her to find her target, namely the alcove booth occupied by the president and CEO of the network and his execrable niece. Having spotted them, she affected her best smile–which in truth was as grotesque as a Neiblubian death-mask–and swam silently up to their table.

"Oh, hello dear Elvie! You didn't tell me you were Mr. Camford's niece during our brainstorming session this morning. You are as modest as you are beautiful, my dear!"

Please indulge me for a moment as I present a description of Rufus Camford. He was almost certainly the most powerful man in the business, with favors owed him from one end of the galaxy to the other. It was said that, with a single phone call, he could create careers *ex nihilo* or even resurrect them from the dead. It was he who, singlehandedly, had revived the company's struggling theme park business a decade ago. He who had secured the intellectual property rights to *Star Attack* and brought it's almost cult-like following into the fold. He who had overseen the highest ratings in network history. In short, Rufus Camford was a living legend. What's more, he had managed all of this without so much as a whiff of scandal to his name, for he was a gentleman. A throwback to a bygone era, some said, when a handshake was as good as an ironclad contract and a secret shared in confidence might as well have been deposited into a black hole. He was kind, generous, always polite, and - most astonishingly of all - humble. An all-round mensch.

"That's my Elvie, all right," beamed Camford. "I practically had to beg her to come to work for us, so intent was she not to trade on her family connections!"

Elvie flushed with embarrassment, for all around the cafeteria the clownfish were poking out of their anemones, the crabs were lifting a curious eye above the sand, and the octopi were turning garish green with envy.

"Marvelous!" said Neezquaff. "Absolutely splendid! Your niece and I were discussing her thoughts about the show just this morning, and I could tell immediately that I was in the presence of budding genius. In fact, Elvie, I should be delighted if you would come up to my office later this afternoon to continue our conversation. Writers' rooms are pits of despair, after all, and a resplendent bird such as yourself should be allowed to soar freely above the clouds, with the wind at your face and the sun upon your back!"

"What do you say, Elvie?" asked Uncle Camford. "That sounds like quite an opportunity. You may not know it, but Betty Neezquaff is a star in her own right, a real force to be reckoned with. And she doesn't give such praise lightly."

Elvie, who was both unaccustomed to such flattery and grounded enough to see through it, merely nodded.

"It is a date, then!" said Neezquaff. "I will have Edwina put an invite on your calendar. Oh, and Elvie…it would be prudent not to tell the other writers about this. They're a bitter and jealous lot to begin with and would surely seek to make you suffer for the crime of rising above their mediocrity. Toodle-oo!"

Camford could scarcely contain his pride. "How about that, dear niece?" he said. "Less than a week on the job, and you've already got Body Count Betty wrapped around your finger. And I had nothing to do with it! Remarkable!"

He dived back into his salad with renewed vigor while Elvie contemplated the exchange. On many planets–including Elvie's–there are ancient myths that warn against rising too high, too fast. In all of them, the naive protagonist's aspirations end in disaster, a cautionary example against unchecked ambition. But despite her gentle nature, Elvie was not naive. She knew that Neezquaff was up to no good and that the slightest misstep could send her tumbling to earth with a great thud.

"Yes, Uncle," she said. "It is remarkable indeed. I can't imagine what someone of Ms. Neezquaff's stature would find interesting about me. Perhaps it has something to do with my question to her this morning."

"Oh, and what question is that?" asked Camford.

"I wondered if it might be the kind and decent thing to evacuate the Rexans before they are all burnt to carbon dust by the rogue star?"

At this, Rufus Camford wiped his mouth, put down his fork, and looked keenly upon his treasured niece.

"A happy ending, then?"

"Well...yes, I suppose so," said Elvie. "And let's not forget billions of lives saved in the bargain."

"My dear, sweet Elvie," he began. "In all my long years in this business, that may be the best idea I have ever heard! After all, what good is a story if it doesn't have a happy ending? We are not in the business of depressing people after all. Not only is it bad for ratings, our advertisers can't abide it. And what did old Body Count have to say about this suggestion of yours?"

"She didn't seem too keen on it, if I'm being quite honest," said Elvie with her typical forthrightness.

"Hmmm...yes, I see," replied the mogul. "Well, that does complicate matters. It sounds like you have some work to do to convince her. I can't very well just swoop in and overrule the hottest showrunner in the industry. That wouldn't reflect well on either of us."

"I shall do my best, Uncle," said Elvie. And she meant it.

CHAPTER 5

Though it was one day closer to the end of the world, chez Obgulagong had never known a brighter morning. Gumpilos was singing merrily to himself as he prepared omelets while Cniphia luxuriated in post-coital bliss.

When the folded egg dishes were ready, Gumpilos plated them and poured two cups of coffee mixed with blorkin milk. To his delight, he found in Cniphia's refrigerator a healthy sprig of parsley, which he promptly clipped and used as a garnish for the omelets.

After floating into her room as if on a cloud, he gently kissed her on the forehead.

"I've made brekkie for us. Will you take it in bed or in your salon?"

"But in bed, of course!" said Cniphia, unaware that she was already beginning to pick up some of Gumpilos's quirky but charming diction.

"Back in a jiff," rejoined her suitor. And so he was, returning just a few seconds later and to place a table tray, laden with the lovingly-prepared food, upon her blanketed legs with the utmost care.

As is so often the case when food is prepared lovingly on one's behalf, the omelets were the most delicious Cniphia had ever tasted. Perfectly seasoned, with a fluffy quality ideally proportioned to their size and–most impressively–no excess of melted cheese oozing out through its folds like the innards of a squashed bug.

"Cor!" she said finishing the last bite. "That was the dog's bollocks."

Gumpilos seemed as tickled by the compliment as he had been by her romantic ministrations the night before, and he leaned over to plant a kiss square on her mouth.

"As are you, my dear! Well, it is a beautiful Saturday outside. What do you think we should do?"

From another man, Cniphia might have suspected that this was no more than a sly invitation to stay indoors and continue the previous evening's activities. But she realized immediately that Gumpilos was completely sincere, and this prompted in her an unexpected crisis of confidence.

Have you ever noticed how anxious thoughts are much like a ludicrously elaborate domino arrangement, starting out with a few seemingly harmless wobbles and then, before you know it, spreading out in a rolling wave of destruction so glorious and well-ordered that one can only stand back and admire its machine-like flagitiousness?

That is what happened to Cniphia. A thought occurred to her, an unproductive but all-too-common thought she had harbored since childhood. The name of the thought was *I don't deserve this kind of happiness.* It wobbled a bit and then tumbled into an adjacent ideation called *Well, it probably won't last long anyway.* This one, in its turn, knocked down another thought best described as *You've been disappointed before, you daft cow, and yet here you are again, leaving yourself vulnerable to emotional injury*, which toppled a pair of twins whose names were *Your mother was right all along*, and–to mingle the Rexan language with the galactic common tongue–*Mxtlpicam' bnak ooligapn, the end of the world is practically around the corner*. And so it continued, an intricate architecture of mental dominoes that Cniphia had spent a lifetime setting up, knocking down, and carefully replacing in an endless cycle.

Though she despised herself for what she considered to be an appalling display of weakness, she began to cry.

Naturally, this alarmed Gumpilos to the utmost degree.

"Whatever is the matter, my dear?" he asked.

"You don't have to do this, you know," sniffed Cniphia. "You should probably just sod off and enjoy the rest of your weekend. There aren't very many of them left after all."

As we have established, Gumpilos was somewhat lacking in the romantic experience department. Were he some jaded lothario, he might perhaps have recognized her reaction for what it was–fear of commitment combined with a punctured bucket of self-esteem that had been leaking since childhood. Instead, he took it quite literally, and responded with his usual earnestness.

"Why on Rexos-4 would I do that, Cniphia? If I could spend every Saturday I have left–indeed, every remaining minute and hour–with you, I would do so without hesitation." He paused for a moment, for even an unwounded heart must tremble at the words he was about to utter. "Besides which, I love you. And I thought, perhaps, that you might love me as well." He dared to grasp three of her hands as he said this.

"But you don't even know me," she protested. "Not really. It's far more likely that you are in love with the idea of falling in love."

"Do we ever truly know a person before we fall in love?" he responded. "It seems to me that to love someone is to will the good for them, to care deeply about their happiness and wellbeing, and to want always to get to know them better. And that is precisely how I feel about you."

Cniphia couldn't help but laugh through her tears. Her mother, after all, had told her repeatedly as she was growing up that she wouldn't know love if it sneezed in her face, and it was to spite her mother that she had asked Gumpilos out in the first place.

I will not tread upon the sacred intimacy of the conversation that followed by reporting its details, for if one picks a thing apart to its constituent elements, one is bound to lose the all-important gestalt sense of what the thing really *means*. Therefore, dear reader, you will have to be satisfied with the bare facts: Cniphia told Gumpilos all about her unhappy childhood, including the part where her parents had both committed suicide in the Rexan tradition of ennui, leaving her to spend her teenage years in a succession of foster care facilities. She told him about her numerous run-ins with law enforcement over petty crimes and about the endless series of louts she had dated before meeting Gumpilos. She even revealed to him her mother's cruel comment, the one that had prompted her to go out with him.

Through it all, Gumpilos listened intently, blinking only when his own tears threatened to spill out.

"So…having heard my sordid backstory," said Cniphia by way of conclusion, "you will no doubt want to reconsider your position and make alternative plans for the weekend."

"On the contrary," he replied. "Amidst the pathos of your saga, I detected an unbroken thread of hopefulness and strength that is most admirable. I scarcely thought it possible, but I now love you more than I did before."

To her astonishment, Cniphia believed him. Not only because her large brain had already ascertained that Gumpilos was constitutionally incapable of lying, but because she *felt* it– in both of her hearts. Though she had never before experienced the luxury of indulging in sentimental notions such as destiny or true love, she found herself on this particular Saturday morning, just months before the end of all things, sitting atop a veritable dragon-horde of emotional riches beyond her wildest imaginings.

The lovestruck couple spent the rest of the day together, sharing a tempest of personal histories and secret dreams, and laughing more than either of them could remember. As the sun began to lower in the evening sky over the great bay of their city, they ducked into a seafood shack near the waterfront for the evening repast. It was not fancy–the restrooms were labelled "Gulls" and "Buoys," and the walls were adorned with bric-a-brac intended to connote a romantic sea-faring past that had never actually happened, at least in this particular timeline.

When Cniphia returned to the table after visiting the "Gulls" room, she was surprised to find a small cake on the table, with a circle of flickering candles waiting to be blown out. Being a naturally observant–and at times even hypervigilant–person, she noticed the waitstaff casting furtive glances in their direction, and other tables whispering to one another whilst pretending not to look.

Her smile as she took her seat was somewhere between tentative and coquettish.

"What's all this about?" she asked.

"Love," responded Gumpilos. "It is about love, dear Cniphia. I love you, as the saying goes, to the moon and back. This has been without a doubt the greatest day of my life. You may think it rash and numpty of me, but I have concluded that I do not want to spend another moment apart from you as long as our world shall last. I believe, in fact, that we were made for one another. Therefore," he said going down upon one knee, "I humbly but hopefully ask for your hand in marriage. Will you make me the happiest man on Rexos-4?"

A person's life hinges upon certain key moments, and this was one of them. For though there may be many worlds, infinitely accommodating in their variety and branching off in all directions based upon our every "yes" or "no," we can only live in one of them at a time. Here, then, was the hinge of Cniphia's life. These moments are so sacred that even cynics and perfect strangers must adopt an attitude of prayerful silence should they be so fortunate as to witness one. The entire restaurant fell quiet, neither a clink of cutlery nor a gulp of food was heard.

I will not keep you in suspense. Cniphia was no fool, and she immediately agreed to the proposal.

"Yes!" she exclaimed. "Yes, yes, yes! A thousand times yes."

The rest of the restaurant applauded and cheered in eucatastrophic release, whereupon Gumpilos swept Cniphia up into his arms and kissed her mouth repeatedly.

The cake remained uneaten, for the two lovers were keen

to return to Cniphia's flat for a more private celebration of their agreed-upon nuptials. Meanwhile, at the edge of the Rexan solar system, a small moon wobbled out of its orbit and crashed into the embrace of its cold gas giant under the gravitational tumult of the approaching rogue star.

CHAPTER 6

If there was one thing that Betty Neezquaff was known for, it was subverting expectations.

I have already noted how she acquired the sobriquet "Body Count Betty" by introducing mass slaughter into a primetime family sitcom, but believe me when I say that this was just the tip of the proverbial iceberg. Her entire career had been built upon a singular talent for violating every norm of traditional storytelling and doing the exact opposite of what the audience desired.

She had transformed cartoon princesses into entitled bullies, endowed monstrous villains with relatable personality traits, made people laugh out loud at the goriest violence imaginable, and ensured that the bad guys won considerably more than their fair share. Under the Neezquaffian show-running ethos, heroes were revealed as dastardly cynics with appalling private appetites, and paragons of virtue became wanton hussies. I am sorry to say it, but she lived according the primeval Luciferian creed: "Evil, be thou my good!"

In short, no trope was safe in her presence.

All of which made Betty a particularly valuable member of her mafia.

But do not get the wrong idea here, dear readers. Betty Neezquaff was not part of anything so crude as a gang of miscreants who went about demanding protection money from frightened immigrant shopkeepers. Nor, as a general rule, did her group place cement shoes on people before dropping them into deep bodies of water or run card-sharking operations out of the back of restaurants. No, I use the term "mafia" here in the more ecumenical sense.

I don't mean to disillusion you, but the sad truth is that the entire universe is run by mafias of one sort or another. It seems to be rather in the natural order of things. A group of like-minded people gravitate towards one another, organize themselves to varying degrees, and then set about the all-important business of making sure that no one encroaches on their turf. The first mafia was probably a group of single-celled organisms who, upon finding a particularly succulent bit of primal muck, made it their purpose to ensure that other single-celled organisms were kept far away from it.

Peace is generally maintained between the various and sundry mafias by the judicious delineation of territory. What seems a juicy mound of muck to one group may be of little interest to another, with its own mound to protect, and so on and so forth. As long as these boundaries are respected, everyone can commit themselves to the all-important task of making money and winning prestige.

Gallywood, however, is a different story. Perhaps this is because it is the juiciest muck heap of all, positively oozing with money and fame and the like. Here, there can be no peace, for every mafia worth its salt wants a piece of the action.

Neezquaff's faction was one of the most fearsome of all, having risen to prominence by ruthlessly subverting expectations and tropes of all kinds.

Now, anyone who has ever been in a crime syndicate will tell you that the thing you have to watch out for the most is not the predictable and generally ineffectual attacks from outside. Rather, it is the knife in the back, the garotte in the middle of the night, the friendly face of a supposed ally smiling down at you as he calmly deposits a bullet into your brain. A mafia, in short, is held together by fear, not of the other side but of itself.

There was, therefore, only one person in the galaxy whom Betty Neezquaff truly feared, and that was the mysterious

Mr. Kratsch, the head of her order. No one knew his true identity of course, but a mere phone call from him was enough to fill even the most steely-eyed bully with dread.

It is important for you to know these things lest you think that the buck stopped with Betty, so to speak. She was but a capo. An effective one to be sure, but still utterly dependent upon the good graces of her benefactors and co-conspirators.

The naked truth was that she had little interest in *What's the Bloody Point?* and, before being brought in, had seen only a handful of episodes, against which she had inveighed profanely over her usual nightcap of Khorgan blood wine and quaaludes.

Thus, the position she now occupied, though coveted by every ambitious up-and-comer in Gallywood, was but a stepping stone, a tedious but necessary waystation on her way to the ultimate target: *Star Attack*.

Oh, how she and her cohorts loathed that franchise, full as it was of undisturbed traditional archetypes that followed the pattern of the Hero's Journey. It was a ripe, lush fruit waiting to be subverted and yet dangling forever just beyond their reach.

One man stood between them and their ambition, and that man was Rufus Camford.

Camford, as we have said, was an executive of the *ancien regime*. He preferred his heroes unsullied, his endings happy, and his expectations met, thank-you-very much! It was also he who had acquired the rights to *Star Attack* from its creator a decade before, and he stood athwart its gates like an adamantine paladin forever saying to would-be subverters and ret-conners "You shall not pass!"

It galled Neezquaff that this hidebound dinosaur should be such an obstacle.

But, as we have already discussed, one does not rise to a perch so high as the one occupied by Body Count Betty by being impulsive. And so she lurked and waited and bided her time, confident that the powerful oppressor would eventually be removed from her path, whether it be by the vicissitudes of biology or by corporate politics. She was always on the lookout for any opportunity to be the agent of her own destiny.

On this day, she considered all the dark prayers she whispered into the night to have been answered, for destiny had delivered her salvation in the form of a simpering, veal-faced goblinette who happened to be the cherished niece of her nemesis.

The vexatious gamine was already a full minute late for their meeting. *Late! For a meeting with Betty Neezquaff!* She smacked her lips, dreaming of torments that would make the lowest demons of Hell say, "Right then, don't you think that may be a bit much? Perhaps we ought to dial it back a bit."

Her eldritch reverie was interrupted by the fastidious voice of her assistant over the intercom.

"Ms. Renfro is here to see you ma'am. Shall I send her in?"

"Immediately," said Neezquaff, making a mental note that Edwina, too, would one day feel the righteous, thermonuclear heat of her wrath.

Moments later, Elvie Renfro harrowed her door. Neezquaff welcomed her with the punctilious courtesy a spider might show to a fly.

"Do come in, dear, and make yourself comfortable!"

That was of course quite impossible. Elvie was a good person, and no good person could possibly feel comfortable in an office which smelled vaguely of sulfur and was filled with menacing and angular pieces of modern art along with various monuments to Neezquaff's prestige.

Elvie eschewed the black-and-red pleather sofa, upon which a number of unholy rites had taken place, and sat instead upon the simple chair in front of Betty's desk.

A short and awkward silence passed, filling the space normally occupied by obsequious bowing and scraping by whomever happened to be sitting in Elvie's place. Neezquaff parted the dead air first, peering down at her junior over cat-eyed glasses that, on some people, might look grandmotherly but somehow only accentuated her predatory features.

"So...about this morning. Surely you understand that I

can't show any favoritism towards you in front of those slack-jawed dunces in the writers' room. You should take it as a compliment that I even took the time to respond so thoughtfully to your proposals."

Elvie did not keep a running tab on such things, but she was fairly certain that Neezquaff had insulted her at least ten times during the morning's exchange. In truth, it was twice that number owing to the fact that the showrunner had a special talent for embedding insults within insults. But, as you know by now, Elvie was as focused and determined as a bulldog playing tetherball, so she simply said, "Of course, Ms. Neezquaff. I value constructive criticism above all other forms of feedback."

"Right. So, let us pick up where we left off then, shall we?"

For a moment, Elvie braced for another volley of imprecations concerning her physical appearance, but quickly deduced that Neezquaff wanted to talk about the show instead.

"That would be lovely," she replied.

"I've been thinking more about what you said. Your exact words escape me, but it was something along the lines of blah, blah, blah we should do something to help the poor Rexans, yada-yada."

Elvie nodded her head in agreement with the summary, which—though lacking in detail or compassion—was broadly accurate.

"Now, normally I am all for keeping the talent on a short leash," Neezquaff continued. "You have to be severe with these people or they start to become big-headed. A good public execution has its uses—I once fired the female lead in a romantic comedy midway through filming just to send a message. And don't get me started about the union. If you give them an inch, they'll take a light year, believe me. However, in this particular instance, your humanitarian instincts happen to coincide with my vision for the conclusion of this program…"

"Oh!" said Elvie. "So we are going to save them, then?" She could scarcely believe her good fortune.

"But of course we are, my dear! I have been looking

for a way to pull together all of the humbly-jumbly storylines and subplots into something that works as a coherent whole. Besides, it is a deliciously subversive conclusion to what has been–let us be honest–a rather predictable and jejune run. I predict that the ratings will be higher than ever. Hark at me! Who would ever expect *me* to preside over a happy ending?"

Elvie did not approve of Neezquaff's less-than-altruistic motives, not for one Rexan second, but any discomfiture on her part was more than offset by the outcome, about which she was chuffed as nuts.

"And, since this was your idea, sweet girl, I want you to oversee the storyline. You will be in charge of the writers' room from this moment forward! How does that sound?"

"Gosh, Ms. N. I don't even know what to say. It sounds almost too good to be true."

Dear reader, I probably needn't tell you this, but it sounded too good to be true because it was too good to be true, for reasons that will become apparent momentarily.

Neezquaff placed her elbows on the desk and perched her chin upon her ghoulish fingers. Elvie fought an internal battle in her hindbrain against a primal instinct that urged her to flee before it was too late.

"It's a pity we can't save them all," said the executive airily, pursing her lips together in a grotesque pantomime of sympathy.

Now, Elvie was no fool, and realized almost immediately that she was being played. It was to her credit that she remained calm in the face of adversity.

"I'm sorry…what do you mean when you say that we can't save them all?"

Neezquaff feigned shock, even going so far as to place a hand over the place where her heart would have been if she had one.

"Surely you didn't think we could organize the evacuation of an entire planet of five billion souls in just a matter of weeks? The logistics of such an operation would be…

well, impossible. And that's to say nothing of the costs! Even I–Betty Neezquaff–do not have an unlimited production budget!" Of course this was a lie, for she had specifically negotiated an uncapped budget prior to taking the job.

"But...well...then what do you propose? How many of them can we save?"

"Excellent questions, my dear. Your uncle is fortunate to have such a brilliant and beautiful niece! I shall answer the second question first. We can save 100,000 Rexans. Isn't that marvelous?!"

Elvie was no mathematician, but she was possessed of one of those extraordinarily plucky minds that rises to the challenge of the moment. And by doing so, she quickly calculated the alarming bleakness of Betty's numbers.

"So...we're going to save just one out of every fifty thousand people, then?"

"If you say so," said Neezquaff. "Unless, of course, you would prefer that we let them all be cruelly snuffed out in a stellar fireball?"

There are small-brained fish living at the bottom of vast oceans which have, over untold millions of years, evolved a single, but essential skill: that of dangling a small bit of bait just in front of their mouths. It could be a little worm-like piece of extraneous flesh or a phosphorescent bulb visible for miles in the lightless void. Either way, it served its purpose, which was to entice other fish to approach close enough to make for an easy meal. One cannot blame the other fish for falling for this trick nearly every time. It is in their nature, so to speak. They have been designed in such a way as to make the vermicular appendage or softly glowing orb irresistible.

So it was at this moment between Elvie and Neezquaff, with the former playing the role of the ill-fated quarry and the latter being the bottom-dwelling harbinger of death. The predator had set the bait and had only to wait for poor Elvie to swim near enough.

"Very well," said Elvie, who knew perfectly well that she

was already in the belly of the beast. "It is better to save one hundred thousand than none at all. How do you propose we do this?"

"I can think of nothing more fair-minded than a planet-wide lottery" replied Neezquaff. "It will make for spectacular television! Just think of it, Elvie–we shall appear as angels of hope and deliverance to the poor benighted Rexans."

"I suppose we will, at least to those fortunate enough to be selected," muttered Elvie, who was feeling quite deflated despite the prospect of her saving 100,000 lives. "I'd better return to the writers' room–they'll be wondering where I am…"

Neezquaff, having just swallowed her meal whole, had already moved on to other business during the digestive phase and spoke without bothering to look up from her terminal.

"Oh, one more thing before you return to the dungeon. I have arranged a makeover for you. Hair, nails, skin, teeth, clothes–the works. I can't have you looking like…well, like you do. Not now that you're one of my rising stars." The monitor screen reflected brightly against her spectacles, lending her a demonic air. "Edwina will escort you to the executive spa and provide you with anything you need as the new lead writer for the *What's the Bloody Point?* Now, get out of my office."

CHAPTER 7

Having agreed to spend the remainder of their days in matrimonial bliss, Gumpilos and Cniphia saw no reason to delay their gratification. The wedding took place a mere week or so after the marriage proposal at the fish shack.

The event was a modest affair, attended by only a few of their co-workers as well as Gumpilos's parents, who–it must be said–were characteristically supportive of their son's headlong plunge into matrimony.

In another timeline perhaps, one in which they might have placed their daughter's happiness above their own self-indulgent world weariness, Cniphia's parents too watched their daughter take her sacred vows.

The newlyweds honeymooned in the traditional Rexan style, at a tropical resort in an archipelago of windswept islands that were encircled by reefs and an armada of cruise ships swollen with bucket-listers taking advantage of the favorable apocalypse pricing.

On the morning before they were scheduled to return home, Gumpilos opted to go snorkeling while Cniphia, whose iridescent skin was more susceptible to sunburn, remained in their suite.

The reef was particularly active that morning, with a mesmerizing kaleidoscope of multi-colored fish darting about the water, blissfully unaware that they would soon be boiled alive as the seas of Rexos-4 came to be evaporated by the rogue star. Gumpilos took in the scene, his mind occupied with thoughts of how he would describe it to his bride, for he had forgotten to bring the disposable underwater camera despite her several reminders.

Though he had only been asea for an hour, Gumpilos was surprised to find the beach, which had been teeming with activity when he entered the water, completely abandoned. Still wearing his flippers, he tramped across the wet, compacted sand at the ocean's edge and into the powdery stuff above the water line, wondering if he'd perhaps missed the announcement of a spontaneous luau or the sighting of a burr-shark.

In the pool area, he followed a breadcrumb trail of discarded drink umbrellas to the tiki bar, where a large group of people had gathered around the teevee.

"What's all this, then?" he asked a fearful-eyed female who was absently holding two empty Mai Tai glasses. Instead of responding, she allowed both glasses to slip from her fingers and hurried towards a poolside room on the first floor.

Gumpilos noticed that the bar's television was tuned to a twenty-four-hour news channel, which had recently abjured its usual bilious programming in favor of a long-form documentary called *Rexos-4: A Retrospective*. He could immediately see by the grave face of the reporter–not to mention the rapt attention of his fellow vacationers–that something was terribly amiss.

Elbowing and apologizing his way through the crowd, he eventually got close enough to be able to hear the audio feed.

"...the alien contact is undoubtedly the most significant event in the history of Rexos-4, and it couldn't come at a better time, just months ahead of our long-expected apocalypse. Back to you, Jane."

The image switched over to the anchor, along with a photo featuring one of the most hideous-looking creatures Gumpilos had ever seen, an eldritch horror straight out of Rexan children's nightmare. Beneath the photo were the words "Betty Neezquaff."

"The message from the alien emissary, which came through just forty-five minutes ago, appears to be one of peace and even hope. It spoke of a galactic civilization that was aware of our, er, predicament and seemed to suggest that some kind of intervention may be in the offing."

At this, the dodgy alien, whom Gumpilos had assumed to be a Betty Neezquaff (or perhaps just a Neezquaff whose name was Betty), began to speak in halting but passable Rexan.

"We have been watching your planet with great interest for quite some time now," it said. "Perhaps we should have called sooner, but as the saying goes, 'better late than never.'" It then made a rude facial gesture, baring its teeth and lifting up the corner of its ghastly mouth, drawing more than a few gasps of horror from the vacationers. Gumpilos ascertained that this was a clumsy attempt at a smile.

"At any rate, we come in peace. And while there's not much we can do about the star presently gobbling up your solar system, we do sincerely want to help as best we can. Therefore, we will be evacuating one hundred thousand Rexans and relocating them to suitable accommodations on other planets, space permitting. Spots on the evacuation star-busses will be allocated based on a planet-wide lottery. I stress that there is no need to fill out any entry paperwork, as we have records of every member of the cast–er, I mean your species–on file. We are working out the logistics–which are a bit more challenging than you might think–and we hope to announce the lucky winners within the next month or so. In the meantime, I encourage you to carry on with your usual hijinks and escapades. Toodle-oo!"

The news anchor affected the grim solemnity common to all practitioners of that profession, but Gumpilos thought he could detect, just beneath the surface, the pep of someone who was simply delighted to be back in the game.

"And there you have it, Rexans," she said. "The first contact from an alien species. A message of hope, at least for some. Coming up next, a panel discussion with various luminaries on what this all means, but first, a word from our sponsors." The television quickly cut to a jaunty little ditty promoting a breakfast cereal so delicious that it cannibalized itself in gruesome fashion, and the small crowd around the tiki bar began to disperse.

Gumpilos removed his flippers and raced back to the suite.

In his frenzied state, he fumbled with the electronic key long enough that Cniphia opened the door for him from the inside. She had been watching a different news channel, for they had not been married long enough for their tastes in media to converge.

"Can you believe it?" she gasped.

"Hardly! It seems almost too good to be true!"

Together, they listened once again to the message from the Neezquaff, switching off the set only when the coverage pivoted to an analysis of the alien creature's fashion.

"I'm not sure I like the look of that thing," said Cniphia.

"I am quite sure that I don't!" replied Gumpilos. "But then beggars can't be choosers, I suppose."

"No, I don't suppose they can..."

"And I'm sure we aren't winning any beauty pageants according to their standards, either," he continued

"No, probably not." Something in her manner suggested she wasn't fully buying it.

"What's wrong, dear?" asked Gumpilos. "Surely this must be good news–or interesting news at the very least. These aliens showing up might give us some hope at just the right moment."

"Don't you find it all a bit...suspicious?"

Cniphia's question was rather hypothetical, given that Gumpilos rarely found anything to be suspicious. His nature was to take good news at face value.

"I find it improbable, I suppose, but I wouldn't call it suspicious," he countered. "What's worrying you?"

"She explicitly said that they had been watching us, Gumpilos. 'For quite some time' were her words. I mean, isn't that a bit creepy? I'd almost call it voyeuristic."

"Well, they are hyper-advanced aliens after all. I should imagine they do a lot of observing and monitoring of primitive species. No doubt for noble and high-minded purposes. Research and whatnot. It's not like they're beaming us up into spacecraft and probing us."

Cniphia suppressed a shudder.

"It's just…I don't know. It feels a bit ill-mannered, doesn't it? I mean, why not just knock on the door, so to speak, and say 'Hullo, we're a galactic civilization, and we'd like to invite you to be a part of it' as opposed to all this skulking around and 'observing?'"

"I think you are overreacting," said Gumpilos. "And besides, isn't that what they're doing now? Better late than never, yes, Cniphia?"

But she was distracted, one might even say agitated, and was busily looking around the room in search of some hidden camera. Gumpilos noticed that her pupils were moving from left to right in a most dramatic fashion.

"They could be watching us even now," she said in a raspy whisper.

CHAPTER 8

A slight shiver ran down Elvie's spine, and she quickly turned off the feed.

Although she was now a television executive and had realized even at the precocious age of four that the people on the screen could not, in fact, see her as she saw them, Cniphia's comment still unsettled her. It made her feel rather like a voyeur. Made her question the ethics of the whole enterprise, in fact.

Many of the brainiest scientists claim that the entire universe is but a mere holographic wave-function and that everything in it exists in a Hilbert space of near infinite possibilities until the moment that it is observed. A cat in any given box may be dead or alive or quite possibly both until someone lifts the lid and looks inside. So intimate is the relationship between observer and the observed that they can scarcely be said to be independent of one another.

Sports fans intuited this long before physicists, and have therefore developed an elaborate set of rituals governing their intake of key moments in important contests. They know perfectly well that wearing certain lucky socks, chanting certain words of encouragement, or watching certain events through a bramble of fingers can in fact project a spooky action at a distance, at times dramatically altering outcomes.

Over the past few weeks, Elvie had become quantumly entangled with Gumpilos and Cniphia due to her keen interest in their storyline. At odd moments during the day, she found herself wondering what the improbable couple might be up to and checked in on them the way a nicotine addict might duck out for a quick ciggie. Because we live in an appallingly pornographic age, I hasten to say that her interest was in no way prurient–on the few occasions when she had accidentally tuned in during moments of their physical intimacy, she always killed the feed, even going so far as to whisper apologies that the Rexan lovebirds would never hear.

Nevertheless, such entanglements do pose established dangers for entertainment executives in general, and for writers in particular. Those who must live according to the creed of "kill your darlings" become attached to specific characters or storylines at great peril to themselves. If anything, this is even more true when it comes to reality programming, where at least in theory anything can happen to anyone at any time. And I'm sure I needn't tell you about the folly of becoming attached to characters living under the doom of a fiery apocalypse.

Elvie Renfro, however, was a caring and decent person first and a writer-cum-assistant producer second. And because caring and decent people are drawn to each other across time and space by a force more powerful than gravity, her attraction to the Tfliximop couple was in a sense inevitable.

All of this is to say that Cniphia was quite right–they *were* watching. Elvie, as we have just stated, but also many other interested parties, including Betty Neezquaff.

And if caring and decent people are therefore drawn to one another by destiny's gentle gravity, then we must sadly conclude that there are also less felicitous forces at work in the universe. Just as burr-sharks are said to be able to sniff out a single molecule of blood in millions of cubic tons of seawater, narcissists and other psychic predators can detect vulnerable wholesomeness across light years of distance.

Neezquaff, being a highly evolved predator, was especially sensitive to such perturbations, which to her were an invitation to gratuitous cruelty. It was always delicious to subvert expectations, but to also corrupt innocence in the process? That was too delectable for words!

There is, however, some consolation to be found in this knowledge. Even if she had not been spying on Elvie, gleefully noting the girl's bond with the Tfliximops, Betty Neezquaff would likely have found Gumpilos and Cniphia through her own diligence.

At any rate, Neezquaff happened to turn her feed on at the exact moment that Elvie had turned hers off. She hit rewind and scanned the morning trades as the on-screen Gumpilos scampered backwards from the hotel room to the tiki bar and finally into the Rexan ocean in his flippers, looking even more ungainly than usual.

So far as Body Count Betty was concerned, this was shaping up to be a very good morning. The First Contact message she recorded was delivered just on time and the trades were adrip with unctuous praise for the shocking new direction of *What's the Bloody Point?* And, best of all, the odious little brat-niece of Rufus Camford was the subject of the accolades:

"Rising New Star in Gallywood Ready For Her Close-Up!" cried *Entertainment Digest*.

"Show Business Is Family Business as Camford Niece Takes the Reins," exclaimed the *Gallywood Reporter*. "Triumphant Intro for Renfro!" exclaimed *Hotch-Potch Magazine* in screaming thirty-point font.

And a carefully-airbrushed photograph of Elvie, right next to her Uncle Rufus, appeared alongside the headlines.

Neezquaff spread them all out across her desk and smiled, much in the manner of an ancient commander looking down from a hilltop as his infantry and archers moved into position.

You are no doubt wondering why all of this adulation directed towards Elvie over what was –let us be honest– a rather mawkish narrative pivot should delight her so.

Shall I tell you, or shall I keep you in suspense?

Alas, I fear I have sketched Ms. Neezquaff's character a bit too finely to surprise you with a final-act reveal. She was of course delighted because she had hatched a plot, a wonderful, awful plot of which this was but the opening gambit.

After watching the Tfliximops' brief conversation, she leaned back in her chair and steepled her hands, imitating a gesture popularized by the main villain in the original *Star Attack* trilogy, who was in fact her secret role model.

She even allowed herself a small cackle. "All is proceeding as I have foreseen…"

A click on the intercom followed by Edwina's rebarbative voice snapped her out of it.

"Ms. N, I'm sorry to interrupt your concentration time, but Ms. Renfro is here to see you. Shall I tell her to come back later?"

"No – send her in." It was far too early to gloat, of course, but that didn't mean she couldn't have some fun with the toad-faced little urchin who, despite the ministrations of Gallywood's finest hair and makeup artists, remained as minging as a liver-flavored biscuit.

"Elvie, my dear–it seems you are the belle of the ball! I've just been reading your press clippings from today's trades. Your uncle will be so proud of you and your lottery idea looks to be a hit!"

"Actually, the lottery was your idea, Mrs. N. — I wanted to save everyone if you recall."

God, but this dolorous sack of flesh could suck the fun out of an orgy, thought Neezquaff. The thought caused her to recall the last one she'd attended, and she had to gather her thoughts before continuing.

"That's right, so it was, and so you did. Well, then you may think of me as your fairy godmother! You just do the wishing, my sweet, and I shall accomplish the rest."

"Now that you mention it," said Elvie, "I do have a request."

"For my rising protege? Anything!"

"I was wondering if I might be able to visit Rexos-4?" Elvie continued. "I feel as if my spending time amongst the people there might help me to get a better sense of their culture and therefore add to the verisimilitude of the show. And..." Here she swallowed hard, for she had learned that any display of vulnerability in front of Neezquaff was as the waving of a red cloak before a raging bull. "—And I thought also that I might be able to help them somehow."

If the Devil himself had appeared from a puff of sulfurous smoke in Betty's office to grant her a wish in exchange for her immortal soul, this was not the first one she would make, though it would have been on the short list.

Neezquaff's plot, like all great Gallywood intrigues, was in essence quite simple. It involved the preliminary business of building up Elvie as the latest *enfant terrible* on the scene. This was easily accomplished with a few discreet calls to Neezquaff's flunkeys at the trade publications, who were ever eager to trade their vestigial journalistic integrity for the favor of an industry Fuhrer such as herself.

In issuing her directives, Neezquaff had stressed the importance of emphasizing Elvie's familial connection to Rufus Camford, for it was the mogul – and not his sugar-coated turdlet of a niece – who was her true target.

Once Elvie was established as the brains behind the operation, the next step would be to play the role of secret saboteur, ensuring that any small mistakes multiplied and snowballed until it became evident to all that the snaggle toothed hemorrhoid was in over her head. At this point, of course, all that would remain would be for Neezquaff herself to step in, correct the ship's course, and subvert the expectations of every sentient life form in the galaxy.

Now, it is a fortuitous aspect of creation that the most devilish people generally lack imagination; that part of their brain is otherwise preoccupied with ambition and selfishness. Murder, therefore, had not previously occurred to Neezquaff as a possibility. Presented now with the opportunity to indulge the most mortal of sins, she seized her chance.

"A visit to Rexos-4, you say? Well, that could be a bit

dangerous, sweetling. Are you quite sure that it's a good idea?"

Elvie's face brightened as she seized her opportunity with great sincerity. "I can arrange for Uncle Rufus to send me a pickup ship. And besides, whatever danger I may face is nothing compared to the fiery torments awaiting the Rexans."

The mention of fiery torments was nearly too much for Neezquaff, whose morning had been a veritable embarrassment of sadistic riches.

"Such a brave girl! I shall arrange for your transport to the planet immediately."

"Thank you, Ms. N. I already have my things packed."

CHAPTER 9

Were I more poetically inclined, I might compare what happened next in the marriage of Gumpilos and Cniphia to the improbable flowering of a rose in a desert, or the emergence of a butterfly from its cocoon, or perhaps even a thing with feathers.

It transpired on a morning not long after their honeymoon and the receipt of Rexos-4's first alien transmission.

Gumpilos had already left for the office, having accumulated a pile of past-due orders for time capsules during his absence. Cniphia, it so happened, had the day off from Please Hurry.

Upon rising from their bed, she found that Gumpilos, per his custom, had left her a whole pot of coffee. He'd also left some blorkin butter on the counter so that it might soften enough to be scraped perfectly over her toast. Next to it was a note, addressed to her with a hand-drawn couple of stick-figures whose bodies were in the shape of hearts. It read simply, "Good morning, dearest! I love you more than blorkin butter. -G."

Cniphia smiled and carefully placed the note in a drawer where she saved such things before dropping a slice of seeded bread into the toaster. She poured herself a cup of coffee and noticed her stomach rumbling impatiently as she waited on the toast to pop.

When it did, she placed it on a napkin and smoothed the blorkin butter over it as effortlessly as one draws a hand through water. Outside the kitchen window, a choir of sword-tailed swallows serenaded her as a rosy-fingered dawn crept over a gathering of clouds. Jinks, a cat they had recently adopted, sprang onto the table, rolled onto its back, and stretched regally expecting its belly to be rubbed. In short, the day seemed to be brimming with promise.

Upon taking her first nibble of toast, and without warning, she vomited profusely against the window, sending the swallows off in a huff and generally spoiling the morning's chirpy atmosphere.

In any marriage, there is sure to be a give and take, an ebb and flow, a waxing and waning, as it were, as each partner adapts to the habits and mannerisms of the other. Cniphia was already beginning to pick up not only Gumpilos's diction, but also his deeply ingrained optimism. And so her first thought, optimistically, was that she had just upchucked a piece of undigested fish from last night's dinner. She had meant to retrieve a paper towel with which to sop up the mess, and had almost reached the roll holder only to let loose another volley of barf, this time so forcefully that it ricocheted off the microwave oven door and spattered her face. This so shocked and appalled her that she backed up a little too suddenly and tripped, landing on her fleshy rump with a soft thud. Then, because the universe has a sense of humor, Cniphia vomited explosively across the floor, leaving the kitchen looking as if it had suffered a volcanic mudslide from which she was the sole survivor.

Jinks, who had serenely watched the scene unfold from his tabletop vantage point, now sensed an opportunity to profit from Cniphia's misfortune. After a moment's pause, during which he concluded that no further eruptions were imminent, he leapt down into the glutinous mess and began to lap it up.

They say that slapstick is both the lowest form of humor and the greatest uniter of intellects of varying caliber, and so this episode provoked a wave of laughter from one end of the galaxy to the other. In fact, Cniphia herself couldn't help but laugh, for when one is subjected to such indignity, it provokes an out-of-body experience wherein one floats in the ether like a ghostly spectator.

She considered kenneling the cat to allow herself to clean up the crime scene but thought better of it. *Mxtlpicam' bnak ooligapn...what's the bloody point?* Might as well let the creature enjoy this manna from heaven, since he and his kind would all be extinct in a matter of months. Here, you can see the surprising versatility of the expression.

Fortunately, she had not yet showered. Placing her robe and pajamas into the washing machine–which she set to extra-hot and extra-rinse–she made her way to the bathroom, keeping a protective hand on her stomach the whole time.

The steaming hot shower did not make her feel much better, though the impulse to vomit had mercifully receded. So she returned to her bed, closed her eyes, and tried to think of happy, non-emetic thoughts, whereupon an explanation hit her like a proverbial ton of bricks: she was pregnant!

This, dear reader, is precisely the happy eventuality referenced at the beginning of the chapter!

Yes, without question, Cniphia was pregnant. She could not have been more certain of this had an angel annunciated it in the foyer. She and Gumpilos were going to have a child!

Depending on your planet of origin, you are perhaps wondering about the timing involved. On most planets, the gestational period for an evolved life form ranges from six to ten months, which would put the new Tfliximop's birthdate sometime after their planet had been obliterated. Ubrakians of course remain in utero for nearly a century, but in this, as in most things, they are the exception that proves the rule. However, by a peculiarity of Rexan evolutionary history, members of their species were born a mere month after conception!

Cniphia was still lying in bed and smiling at the ceiling while psychosomatically fighting her nausea when she heard a rustle at the front door. Gumpilos, it transpired, had returned home for lunch.

"Crikey!" she heard him exclaim, having no doubt

discovered the cat feasting on her vomit. "It's like the exit to the bloody Tilt-a-Whirl in here! Cniphia, dear! Is everything alright?"

"Better than alright," she called. "Come to the bedroom, and I'll tell you why."

"I'll be there in a jiff!" came the reply.

Seconds later, Gumpilos rounded the corner into their bedroom in a state of half-undress, having misinterpreted her previous statement as an invitation to engage in matrimonial intercourse.

That thought nearly brought the chunder up once again, so Cniphia sat up quickly in bed and outstretched her hand in a gesture that meant, "Keep your shorts on" in both the literal and figurative sense.

"What ho! Can you at least tell me what's going on?" asked Gumpilos, genially confused.

"Come, husband. Sit by me," said Cniphia, patting the mattress beside her.

Gumpilos sat on the edge of the bed and leant in towards her, his facial expression one of spousal concern.

"Place your hand on my belly," she said, whereupon he did as he was instructed.

As I have already pointed out, Rexan pregnancies are unusual in the rapidity of their progress. Already, the nascent Tfliximop was flopping about inside Cniphia's womb like a seal performing tricks.

"Can this be? Truly?" cooed Gumpilos, beaming.

"Given certain activities that have transpired between us of late, I should say so," said Cniphia, sounding more like her husband than ever.

Gumpilos giggled with unadulterated glee and was about to plant a kiss on Cniphia's forehead when the most remarkable thing happened–an alien materialized in their bedroom! Or rather a holographic image of an alien.

"I hope I'm not interrupting," said the hologram, covering its eyes with its hands, presumably to preserve their modesty.

"Not at all! We're quite decent," said Gumpilos, earning himself an elbow to the ribs from Cniphia. "—Um, what I meant to say was that we were just having a bit of a private conversation. Could you give us a moment, after which we shall be happy to converse with you?"

"Certainly," said the alien before shimmering and dissolving into thin air.

"Right. Now where were we?" asked Gumpilos.

"You mean immediately before we were contacted by some form of alien intelligence?" said Cniphia with great incredulity. "We were discussing the fact that we are going to be parents, which means there will be a lot more vomitous episodes in our lives in the near future. In the interest of getting in some practice, would you mind cleaning up the kitchen? I don't think I can get out of this bed."

"And what about the alien?"

"If it's important, I'm sure she'll call back." Cniphia was the more practically-minded of the two. "She could be a telemarketer of some kind. Now that our planet has been discovered, I'm sure we can expect more of this sort of thing."

"Maybe she's calling to tell us we've won the lottery!" said G. "Wouldn't that just be spiffing!"

"It would indeed, love. Now hurry, before Jinks gorges himself on my puke. We can't be spoiling him or else he will come to expect such treats on the regular."

"With pleasure, madame!" said Gumpilos, kissing her cheek and exiting the room with the exaggerated formality of a vizier retreating from the throne of his sovereign.

By the time he had completed his task and returned to the bedroom, the alien had, in fact, called back and was conversing with Cniphia in a manner so easy, it was as if they had known each other all their lives.

"Oh, Gumpilos dear!" exclaimed his better half. "This is Elvie Renfro. She is en-route to Rexos-4 and was wondering if she might be able to crash with us for a bit when she gets here.

I told her that we'd be delighted to host her first visit to our fair planet."

I have remarked upon how married couples, over a period of time, often adopt one another's characteristics. Cniphia, we have seen, had already begun to absorb some of Gumpilos's sunny openness to new possibilities along with his syntactic quirks. Needless to say, this is a two-way street. Gumpilos, while retaining his innate buoyancy, had come to see the wisdom in Cniphia's more cautious outlook on things. The very recent news that he was to be a father only heightened his newfound sense of prudence. He coughed into his hand.

"Pleasure to make your acquaintance, Elvie Renfro! — Cniphia, might I have a word. In private?"

"Of course! Please take your time" said the alien hologram, which politely vanished.

"Do you think this is a good idea, Cniphia?" asked Gumpilos. "What with you in your condition and whatnot? Seems positively daft if you ask me!"

"My condition?" she said, arching two of her three eyebrows in order to convey her meaning more sharply.

"Oh, dash it–you know what I mean! We've just learned that you are with child, and now you've gone and invited a blooming alien to live under our roof. An alien, I might add, that looks every bit as fearsome as the one who sent the official communique a few weeks back! Besides, we've only just moved in together, and my house is on the smallish side. What will we do when the baby is born?"

"I think she's rather nice," said Cniphia, who prided herself on her ability to judge character. "What's more, I am most disappointed by your reaction. Where is your sense of courtesy, of hospitality? I am surprised, Gumpilos. Surprised and saddened. This is not the man I married!"

"People must be allowed the space to change and grow!" protested Gumpilos. "Besides, I'm to be a parent now, a responsibility I apparently take rather more seriously than you!"

And so it went for several minutes as the newlyweds

conducted their first argument, which ended, as you no doubt will have guessed, in a decisive victory for Cniphia.

To their surprise, the alien reappeared just a minute after the final figurative bell had rung.

"Elvie Renfro," began Gumpilos. "Forgive my surprised and discourteous reaction a few minutes ago. We would of course be delighted to have you stay with us for as long as you wish. Or until the apocalypse. Whichever comes first."

"Thank you, Mr. Tfliximop," said hologram Elvie. "I greatly appreciate your generosity, though as a great admirer of yours, I cannot say I am surprised. By the way, congratulations on the baby. I am so looking forward to meeting him or her. My shuttle should arrive mid-afternoon on the morrow. No need to pick me up. I know where you live of course."

"How exciting!" Cniphia enthused once the alien had disappeared again.

Loath as he was to resume their dispute, Gumpilos felt compelled to object.

"Exciting? There is more here than meets the eye, that is for certain. How did she know about the pregnancy, for example? And how does she know our address? What's more, didn't you find it the least bit uncanny how she just rematerialized the moment we had agreed upon a course of action?" He eyed the air warily he spoke, as if scanning the very molecules for evidence of treason.

"I think you are overreacting," said Cniphia. "Perhaps she is telepathic. As for our address, the first communique said that they had files on all of us. Surely such a database would include our mailing addresses as well as other important details. And she probably just put us on hold–there's no telling what kind of communications technology these aliens might have."

"No telling indeed," muttered Gumpilos, unconvinced and uncharacteristically wary.

CHAPTER 10

Having made contact with the Tfliximops, Elvie at last allowed herself permission to admit what she was truly hoping to accomplish on her visit to Rexos-4: a rescue, if not of the whole planet, then at least of this fledgling family to which she had become so attached.

Unlike Betty Neezquaff, however, she wasn't much of a schemer and as yet had no plan for how she should accomplish her goals. She relied instead upon the innate power of virtue and good intentions, which, as anyone will tell you, are about as useful in the media industry as toilet tissue in a Lorgothan Elephant enclosure.

"Uncle," she said whilst pushing her food about her plate in the commissary. "I've been thinking more about this whole Rexan rescue storyline—"

"Have you," said Camford, who was deeply enthralled with his salad. "And what have you come up with?"

This was not an easy subject to broach, even for someone as innately fearless and unperturbed as Elvie. It was, as they say in the business, a big ask.

"Well, as you know, we are planning on rescuing 100,000 people. Which is very generous, I hasten to add. And yet…"

"…and yet you wish to do more than merely rescue 100,000 Rexans?" said Camford, now more interested in what his niece was saying than in the leafy greens.

"I do. May I pitch you?"

Camford beamed with pride. "Of course, my dear. Pitch

away. Though I must warn you, I prefer to take a hands-off approach on such matters."

"I know you do, Uncle. But hear me out. What if we were to secretly arrange for the rescue of not just the winners of the lottery but of everyone who wants to be rescued? We needn't tell anyone about it–least of all Ms. Neezquaff." Here Elvie shuddered with horror at the reaction the showrunner would likely have to such a development. "We could film two endings, you see. One with just the lottery winners making it out and one with everyone being saved. And you could decide which one to air."

"Hmmmph..." Camford grunted, unconvinced and mentally calculating the extravagant cost of such an approach.

Now she had started, Elvie wasn't going to desist. "I took the liberty of convening a focus group recently, to test the reaction to these different endings."

Camford smiled broadly, for he loved focus groups. Focus groups are natural allies of classical storytelling, of course. Nihilists tend not to show up for them.

"Did you now? And what did you learn?"

"By a margin of four to one, they preferred the ending where everyone gets rescued.

"I have no doubt they did," said Camford, flicking his hand as if batting away a bothersome fly. "The critics, on the other hand..."

Elvie had anticipated this objection.

"No, I don't suppose they will like it at all. But I think that sometimes we defer too much to their tastes, Uncle. I mean, really! They always seem to prefer the most dreadful outcomes, and nobody particularly cares what they think anyway. And what are we in business for if not to entertain and inspire people? Dash the critics, I say!"

This, of course, was the way to Rufus Camford's heart. And if he wasn't already predisposed to agree with his beloved niece, her idealistic defiance of the cognoscenti was enough to persuade him.

"Very well, Elvie. I will arrange it, in secret. But as you

said, no one must find out about this. It would be the ultimate spoiler."

"Oh, thank you, Uncle!" said Elvie, planting a kiss on his cheek. "I've already gotten permission from Ms. N to travel to Rexos-4. But...perhaps you could send a ship to pick me up before the finale?"

"Of course, my dear. And please, be safe."

****

It is a testament to Elvie's altruistic nature that she did not object to flying commercial. That being said, she wondered if Neezquaff had purposefully booked her a middle seat, squeezed as she was between a snoring Oliphoran businessman occupying the aisle and a supercilious fraternity boy from the planet Phi Upsilon by the window. Rebuffing his romantic advances as politely as she could, she closed her eyes to try and get some shuteye, jet-lag on intergalactic flights being bitchier than an erstwhile A-lister who has been relegated to starring in late-night infomercials.

As Elvie drifted off to sleep, she dreamed not of fame and fortune, but of meeting Gumpilos and Cniphia and their offspring.

****

Several million kilometers out from the Rexos-4 system, she was awakened by a stewardess calling her name over the intercom.

"...Elvie Renfro. Will passenger Elvie Renfro please proceed to the Clucker-Chucker terminal at the rear of the cabin? Your departure window will open in five minutes."

As Rexos-4 had no spaceport, Elvie would have to reach the surface of the planet via egg drop. Those of you who have never travelled on a budget may be unfamiliar with niceties of egg-based transportation, which involves being entombed in a small, durable structure (viz. "the egg") which is then filled with a viscous fluid that protects one against such hazards as g-forces, particularly those involved when hitting the surface of a planet at relativistic velocities.

After declining to give the frat-daddy her phone number a final time, Elvie apologetically squeezed past the corpulent Oliphoran to retrieve her carry-on from the overhead compartment. Wheeling it down the aisle, she arrived at the rear of the spacecraft, where she was greeted by the bleary-eyed and somewhat surly stewardess assigned to assist her with eggification.

"Do you have an address?"

"Yes," replied Elvie. "It's 1426 Ickleberry Way, Flatuston-upon-Thongford."

Elvie yolked herself in the center of an egg whose doors were hinged open like a diptych while the stewardess absent-mindedly keyed in her destination. Moments later, the doors closed, encasing Elvie in a gel that smelled vaguely of cigarettes and poverty, through which she could hear a countdown that sounded like a distant whale song.

"…Three, two, one…and drop!"

A portal opened below, and Elvie and her egg were laid into the void of interstellar space, tumbling towards Rexos-4 as the shuttle continued on its journey to a less rusticated destination.

After what seemed an eternity, Elvie felt the azimuth thrusters of the egg kick on, signaling that she was entering the atmosphere. There was a mild thud, followed by a cracking sound, and a slow flowing of albuminous gel out of the egg. Through the crack, Elvie could perceive the claret-colored light of the afternoon sun on Rexos-4. She had landed.

Humdrum as an egg drop might be to the galactic backpacking set, I ask you to imagine how this must all have appeared to Cniphia and Gumpilos, who had just witnessed Elvie's arrival in their back yard. Out of the smoldering wreckage, there oozed a clear-ish slime, which not only soaked their freshly mown lawn but also ran into Cniphia's small garden plot, whereupon the vegetables she had lovingly tended these last few weeks began to wither and turn to ash, egg gel being harmless to sentient life forms but lethal to both legumes and nightshades.

As if this weren't enough, a beakish nose appeared through the crack of the vessel, along with two tiny hands that were attempting to prize it open. Bit by bit, small flakes of the egg's shell fell away, and from its air pocket emerged a short, mostly hairless, alien creature dripping in mucous and blinking its eyes–of which it had but two–as it adjusted to its new surroundings. Where the third eye should have been, there was a mole of some kind with a hair protruding from it.

"Golly," said Gumpilos. And it was to his enormous credit that he did not say more.

Cniphia, too, was taken aback by this unprecedented happening, and though she wouldn't have admitted it, privately wondered if perhaps her husband had been right about this after all.

"Greetings," said the alien, who hastened to add the standard salutation, "I come in peace. My name is Elvie Renfro."

Because of the awkward silence that followed, Elvie wondered if the stewardess had perhaps entered the wrong address.

Cniphia, having gathered her composure and hoping to make a good first impression, strode forward and said rather too loudly, "Greetings, Elvie Renfro! On behalf of our species and those with whom we share a biosphere, we welcome you to Rexos-4. And also to our home."

She then elbowed Gumpilos in the ribs, indicating that he should assist Elvie with her bags, which he set about doing forthwith.

We have not as yet discussed the physiological differences between Elvie's species and the Rexans in any great detail. I shall attend, then, to the particulars of the Tfliximops' reaction to Elvie's appearance.

They noted first the size of her nose. While it was true that Elvie's proboscis was well to the right on the bell curve for her species, Rexans had no noses at all, their olfactory sense instead being fed by small whiskers that curled up reflexively in the presence of malodorous scents and quivered like contented chinchillas when pleased.

Next, they continued to study the alien's near-hairlessness. Again, this is not entirely fair to Elvie, who had more or less the amount of hair nature intended for her. Rexans, on the other hand, were extraordinarily hirsute, both the males and females of the species typically being covered head to toe in wool that ranged from lightly wavy to curly in the extreme and coming in a rainbow of colors.

Finally, there is the matter of size. Elvie of course had the normal stature for people on her planet, but to the Rexans–among whom even a vertically challenged specimen would have been a prized dunkball recruit–she seemed impossibly tiny for an adult.

As for the eyes, well you have no doubt figured that out on your own. Elvie was possessed of just two, which was one fewer than what Gumpilos and Cniphia were used to.

For her part, Elvie had watched more than enough *What's the Bloody Point?* not to be surprised by her hosts, although their height was a bit unexpected. Uncle Rufus had told her that actors were always shorter than they appeared on television.

"Would you like to come inside and freshen up a bit?" asked Cniphia. "I'm sure it was a long trip."

Elvie nodded happily. "A hot shower would be just the thing," she said, attempting to brush some lingering goo from her forearms.

Behind her, the egg smouldered and disintegrated into ash, as they are wont to do after having served their purpose. The neighbor, a sneaky sort of cove who–as fate would have it–happened to be the secret leader of the Rexan Anarchist Party–had surreptitiously observed the reception over a hedgerow. He momentarily considered calling the constable, but thought better of it, when he heard his favorite soap opera come back after the commercial break. *Mxtlpicam' bnak ooligapn. They're never around when you really need them.*

CHAPTER 11

Originality not being her strong suit, Betty Neezquaff had poached the idea for her scheme from a recent installment in the Star Attack franchise, wherein an evil emperor, sensing a threat from a young up-and-coming space knight, had employed all his considerable subtlety to seduce the hero into his service, ultimately sending him on a mission to a doomed planet. There, in the uttermost cave, instead of the magic elixir, the knight found only ash and ruin. He was utterly broken and left for dead by those he had considered his closest friends.

In *Star Attack*, the emperor raced to the planet to rescue his wounded protégé, not out of goodwill, but in order to complete his subjugation of the poor sap, who would now be entirely dependent upon him, not knowing that it was he who had orchestrated the whole affair.

Neezquaff found this last bit predictable and distasteful, not to mention unwise, and she had no intention of repeating the emperor's lapse in judgment. No, Elvie would die on Rexos-4 along with everyone else.

Now, in Neezquaff's defense, originality isn't really everyone's strong suit, least of all in Gallywood. We have already noted the cosmic redundancy of all great poetry, and this–had you been paying close attention–was a bit of foreshadowing of the didactic exposition to which I must now, with apologies, expose you. You are of course free to skip ahead to the riveting action bits and any dramatic sets that might follow, but I am duty bound to tell you that this is the nub of the whole affair. We must pause a moment to discuss the question of tropes.

I take it as given that any reader of this tale is sophisticated and mature enough to realize that stories are not, in fact, real life. Let us face the facts. Real life tends to be a rather dull affair, punctuated of course by moments of bliss or trauma that, taken as a whole, lend a sense of purpose and structure to the otherwise dryly meandering business of sentient existence.

In real life, people are complicated, for the most part. They are painted in what we writers call "shades of grey," meaning that they consist of an equal admixture of good and bad. Now, I rather think that this greyscale aspect of actuality is really rather important. Life would be messy indeed if people, upon emerging from the womb, were sorted into buckets labeled "hero," or "villain," or "guardian," or "wise mentor." On top of that, such a system would deprive people of free will, which, while frequently inconvenient, seems to be the least one can expect from God, given the tall challenges faced by all life in this universe.

And yet, there is something in all of us that yearns for more! A desire, written upon the heart, so to speak, to discover just beneath the surface of everyday existence a hidden structure to things, something more than just turtles all the way down.

I am personally of the belief that this abstraction does exist and that stories are the best evidence of it.

For in stories, you see, we enter into an imaginal realm, which is every bit as real as the realm of the senses. And in this imaginal realm, all things are possible. The shades of grey can be fancified in technicolor brilliance. Purpose and meaning can erupt from the ground like geysers. Ordinary girls can become heroes. Uncles can become wise mentors. Showrunners can live out their fantasies of perfect villainy. And if we can imagine such things, does that not imply that they are wholly possible? It seems to me that anything we can think of is attainable or, to put it another way, the only things that are truly impossible are those we can't even begin to imagine!

And here is the real magic, my friends; good stories have a way of spilling over into what we call real life. In the gunmetal grey of a friend's moral struggle to do the right thing, we catch a glimpse of the rich blues of heroism. Tempting real-life choices, filled as they are with opportunities for self-enrichment, glow with the ruby red of evil itself, warning us to chart another course.

What I have just described is the very basis for Gallywood's existence! It was meant to be a factory of living dreams - the dreaming of which would not only enrich lives but help to color them with purpose. You are probably thinking, *Well, that may be the most Pollyanna thing I have ever had the displeasure of reading. In fact, I think I shall close this book right away and tuck it away with my old copies of 'Space Ranger Junior' magazine and other mementos of childhood.* And, if you are so inclined, there is nothing I can do to stop you. Yet I plead with you to bear with me just a moment longer.

I am not suggesting that all stories must be treacly, or even cartoonish monuments to a fanciful innocence. Far from it! The very best stories are filled with vile vermin doing the worst imaginable things. I am all for blood and guts, ignominy and betrayal, moral turpitude and corruption of all kinds in my stories, provided that they aren't sold to me as something else. To borrow from a common, if rather vulgar, expression, I'd prefer you not to piss down my leg and tell me it's raining.

Indeed, I can even tolerate a certain degree of what the younger generation calls "meta," so long as it is in service of the greater good, which is to say, the business of amplifying dreams and making people's lives marginally better than they might otherwise be!

But the willful subversion of tropes? No, I will not be an accomplice to murder, for that is precisely what it is. I don't care what the critics or the overeducated mid-wits, who command the cultural heights of the moment, say. It is homicidal madness to snipe at the deepest archetypes within our collective subconscious. Worse, it is suicidal! An absolutely dangerous undertaking that, for all its airs of sophisticated nonchalance, is an act of violence against the common good.

Without question, we must have the evil emperor of *Star Attack*, just as we must have the corrupted space knight (who, I must inform you, is given his chance at redemption several episodes later). Indeed, we must have our Betty Neezquaffs and our Elvie Renfros, for without them, what do we have left? Those who say otherwise imagine that they are merely correcting historical injustices and adding complexity and realism, but what they are really doing is draining the imaginal world of all color! In the end, you will Such an undertaking would only serve to render flights of fancy in the same drab grey as our dismal reality, and then where would we be? If reality and dreaming were made the same, then I am certain that both will be the poorer for it.

(I might usher you to one side and further add that the entire enterprise of subverting tropes is doomed to failure from the get-go. Performed often enough, the subversion of tropes becomes a trope in itself after all, but I'm afraid I'm on the cusp of losing you.)

I will conclude thusly: stories are what hold the world together. They accomplish this by the action of love. That is to say, they make us see the world in such a way that it is possible to cherish it. And tropes hold stories together, which means that they are tender and precious things that deserve to be preserved rather than despised, for what sane person would choose nihilism over purpose?

Lack of originality is not a sin. The whole point is not to come up with something completely original–which frankly strikes me as satanically ambitious–but to tell the old stories in ways that are novel, yet respectful.

I daresay that Betty Neezquaff and her ilk will never see it in such a way, but that is almost beside the point. This is my story after all, and in it, Neezquaff is herself a giant, fat, honking trope. In her so-called real life, I'm sure she had one or two redeeming qualities, or perhaps even a touch of guilt or ambivalence about her choices. Let that comfort you if you are of the mindset that villains must be tempered with humanizing characteristics. To be honest, I can't imagine why you would worry about such a thing, especially after having read the past few paragraphs.

At any rate, Neezquaff was feeling rather chuffed at how affairs were proceeding and who could blame her? For Elvie was now stranded on Rexos-4 and out of her hair.

The rogue star was gobbling up matter and disrupting orbits left and right as it careened at the speed of light through the Rexan solar system.

The show had its highest ratings to date.

And best of all, audience expectations had now been set on the most predictable outcome–that Elvie was going to find a way to at least save the now-beloved Tfliximops, and quite possibly the entire planet.

For you see, Neezquaff had engineered it so that Elvie was now part of the show, quite unbeknownst to the girl! She had secretly filmed Elvie's quick breaks to catch up on the Tfliximop family, dramatically scoring it to string music that evoked powerful emotional connections. She had furthermore brought forward the Gumpilos and Cniphia storyline, so that it was practically all anyone was talking about.

"Hey," some citizen would say while gathering 'round the watercooler to discuss the show. "How about that Gumpilos Tfliximop last night on *What's the Bloody Point?* He's a right git, innit?"

To which another might respond, "Actually, I quite like him. He's got an everyman sort of innocence about him that is both charming and relatable in the extreme. I'm rather rooting for him."

"What, that donkey? I can see why you may carry a torch his wife, Cniphia. Smart. Sexy. Really just the bees knees, all round. She could've done soooo much better!"

"Are you daft?" Another would interject. "Her life was an

aimless and pitiful affair until he walked into that coffee shop! Her character has developed quite well since, I'll grant you, but that's mainly on account of Gumpilos!"

And so it would go back and forth until it came to blows or until a managing director, or someone else in authority, would happen by to resolve such disputes with their pearls of wisdom and some iron-fisted diplomacy.

"That's quite enough, you lot!" was a typical admonishment. "It's obvious that they will both be around for at least another season now that Elvie Renfro has shown up. Rufus Camford's own niece! You don't think they'd send her there just to have her fail, do you?"

I can assure you that to have a show discussed in such a way was the highest ambition of every writer in Gallywood. And how envious must those not involved have been to witness *What's the Bloody Point?* being discussed at watercoolers from one end of the galaxy to the other?

Elvie's transit had been the most popular episode in history, just as Neezquaff had predicted. It was all filmed surreptitiously, of course. The fraternity boy, a former intern of Neezquaff's who fancied himself a leading man, had a small camera embedded in the cap he wore backwards on his head.

The Oliphoran businessman? He was a nobody from accounting whom Betty had tapped to play a role in his favorite show. She had given him two extra weeks of paid vacation to sweeten the deal.

Even the stewardess was in on the plot. She was a former administrative aide whom Neezquaff had banished to work for the CEO of an independent art-film studio. Betty had promised to get her a job with a proper Gallywood mogul once again.

Wheels within wheels, plans within plans.

Yes, Betty Neezquaff was quite pleased indeed. And if she felt any misgivings, she certainly did not show it.

CHAPTER 12

While Elvie washed away the grime and despair of commercial shuttle transport and her subsequent arrival by egg, Gumpilos and Cniphia conferred in the kitchen.

"I renew my objection to this project of yours, Cniphia," said Gumpilos. "I am sure she is perfectly nice and mostly harmless, but the fact of the matter is that we have no business hosting an alien during your pregnancy. We have quite enough fish to fry, wouldn't you say?"

Cniphia was no fool and could see the logic of her husband's position, but intuition told her that there was something beyond mere logic at work. So, by way of counterpoint, she settled on a different angle of attack, namely that the *fait* had already been *accompli'd*.

"I won't hear of it, Gumpilos. We have welcomed her into our home, and to go back on that now would be incredibly rude.

"Rude?" replied G. "Why should we be concerned with matters of etiquette where the welfare of our child is concerned?"

Inwardly, Cniphia once again conceded that he had a point and wasn't quite sure how to respond.

However, at precisely this moment, their houseguest rounded the corner with her hands held behind her back so as to conceal something she was holding.

Gumpilos stepped protectively in front of his wife, who privately noted that while it was slightly old-fashioned of him, a bit of chivalry really seemed to have stoked the hot coals of her ardor.

"I have something for you," Elvie Renfro announced. "Well, not for you, actually. For the baby."

And with this, she produced in a flourish that which she had held in secret. It was a stuffed animal with adorably large eyes and a mischievous grin. It was soft and cuddly and smelled like cotton candy bubble gum, though not overpoweringly so. When she handed it to Gumpilos, the little toy exclaimed, "Mxtlpicam' bnak ooligapn!" and giggled to itself.

Needless to say, this magnanimous gesture melted away any remaining doubts on the part of either of the Tfliximops.

"Oh, Elvie Renfro, you shouldn't have!" said Cniphia, stepping out from behind her gallant husband, who at last allowed himself to relax.

Things took a markedly more convivial turn from this point forward, and over dinner, the Tfliximops plied Elvie with enthusiastic questions about the broader universe.

"Gosh—there really is a galactic civilization out there?" asked Gumpilos, "darting around amongst the stars and accomplishing great things?"

Elvie steepled her fingers. "More or less, yes. Mostly, it's just people carrying on about their lives and trying to make their way through the workweek without being discouraged to the point of giving up."

"And you say that you've been…watching us?" asked Cniphia, ever one to get right to the nub of the matter. "But why? And how? What about light speed and relativity and whatnot? I mean, how do you do it?"

Elvie recalled reading in a story once that any sufficiently advanced technology would appear as something rather magical to a more primitive society. This was a good thing, because she hadn't the faintest idea how to explain the technical intricacies of, for instance, the ansible relay network that transmitted information signals via stabilized quantum wormholes, or how a warp drive managed to bend space in front of and behind a vehicle such that spacetime itself acted like a spring. Like most people, she merely took these things as a given, without ever wondering how they actually worked. So she answered as follows:

"Technology and such. You know, science."

Her evasion stirred a final paroxysm of doubt in Gumpilos.

"But that's the problem, you see? I mean, here we are a matter of months away from the end of life as we know it on this planet, and you lot show up suddenly, saying that you've been watching us for years. It seems a bit of a coincidence, you must admit."

Elvie had hoped to defer this conversation for at least a few days, but it was clear there was no way around it. She wiped some Rexan ragout from the corners of her mouth and folded the napkin neatly beside her plate.

"There is something I have to tell you," she started. "There is no easy way to say this, so I'll just come right out with it. You – all of Rexos-4, in fact – have been the subject of the longest-running entertainment program in the known history of the galaxy."

Cniphia blinked all three of her eyes.

"Hey, wait. What do you mean, precisely? Are you saying that we are a television program of some kind?"

"Precisely that."

"And how long has this been going on?"

"A little over 10,000 years. This is to be the final season, on account of…" she suddenly felt quite awkward. "On account of the whole, um, apocalypse business."

Cniphia felt a vortex of outrage rising in her belly, a sensation not dissimilar to her recent bout of pregnancy-induced nausea.

"You are telling us that you people have been watching everything that has happened on this planet for ten millennia, and have only now decided to pay us a visit? With your technology, we might have been able to avoid this coming catastrophe. You might have even been able to save us all!"

Gumpilos wisely remained silent while his wife vented her spleen.

"But we *have* saved you, more than once as a matter of fact," protested Elvie, rather feebly. "We once fixed some faulty plate tectonics that would have resulted in a global tsunami over 1,000 feet high. We helped you find a cure for Tleilax fever. We even intercepted a smallish black hole that would have planted itself in the core of your planet and gobbled it up in its entirety."

"Is that so?" responded Cniphia who had built up quite a head of steam by this point. "And I suppose you expect us to thank you for this, even though you're about to let us be burnt to a bloody crisp by a rogue star?"

Elvie chewed on her lip, fighting the urge to tell the Tfliximops everything, in spite of her uncle's warning.

"I'm told there's nothing we can do about the star," she said, hanging her head. "I'm deeply sorry."

"So what, then? I guess we are some kind of cosmic joke to you. So you're all just going to sit back and watch us melt over a bowl of popcorn?"

"Oh no, it's not like that at all," protested Elvie. "People love Rexos-4, all of you really."

"The wisest man I know once told me that to love someone is to will their good," Cniphia interjected. "It is to care deeply about their happiness and wellbeing, and to want always to get to know them better. The galaxy doesn't love us. They are amused by us. We are objects of entertainment and pleasure for them, nothing more."

She was right, of course. And Elvie knew it. It was, in fact, why she had come all the way to Rexos-4 in the first place. What had started off as mere curiosity had devolved, as curiosity so often does, into guilt. But over time, it had become something much, much more.

"I cannot speak for the galaxy," she said. "Nor can I justify my own part in this. I can only say that I am sorry, truly sorry. And that I do love you, not just you and Gumpilos, but all of the

Rexans. I came here because I wanted to help."

Gumpilos dared at last to put an arm around his wife. Smiling, he said to Elvie, "You know, you seem awfully nice for someone in show business. Here on Rexos-4, they're wankers, the lot of them."

"Oh, it's the same everywhere else, dear Gumpilos," said Elvie. "I consider it to be a mission field. Can you find it in yourself to forgive me, Cniphia?"

The old Cniphia might have held out for a bit, but you know this version of her well enough not to be surprised that her anger had dissolved into a warm smile. She walked around the table and wrapped Elvie in all four of her tentacular arms.

"Of course I forgive you." At that very moment, the little Tfliximop inside her did three flips of joy. "Would you like to feel the baby?" she asked.

"Oh, may I?" cooed Elvie, who was quite a family-oriented person. "Have you thought of a name yet?"

"We're still working on that," said Gumpilos. "Speaking of names, what is this show about us called?"

"Mxtlpicam' bnak ooligapn," said Elvie. "*What's the Bloody Point?* I'm not blowing you off – that is the actual name of the show."

"Ah, well. That checks out," responded her genial host. "It is the great question that has plagued us ever since one of my esteemed ancestors first learned about our inevitable doom. Though lately, I've been thinking about it in a slightly different way..."

"Elvie, dear," said Cniphia. "Do you suppose they are watching us even now?"

Renfro released a sigh. ""Almost certainly. And I do wonder how the audience will feel about my showing up and letting you in on the secret."

The audience, meanwhile, had reacted favorably, to say the least. All around the galaxy, citizens were buzzing with this daring new development. Ratings were through the roof.

"I certainly didn't see that coming, did you?" babbled employees at their watercoolers.

"Well, who would?" others gasped. "It's never been done before in the history of reality TV, breaking the fourth wall like that! Do you suppose they'll tell everyone else on the planet or keep it a secret?"

The general consensus was that the "little princess" would go on to develop a bond with the inhabitants of the doomed planet and then figure out a way to save everyone on it. A happy ending in the truest sense!

"I dunno. But if there's one thing that's clear, it's that we're going to get a happy ending."

"Why d'you say that?"

"C'mon mate! It's so blatant. I mean, the little princess goes to the doomed planet, meets with the locals, develops a bond, and inevitably figures out a way to save everyone. Haven't you been paying attention?"

"'Course I have! But I just watch the show to enjoy it, not as part of some exercise in postmodern meta-narrative media theory!"

"And that's what makes you a perfect bumpkin. Oi, we'd better get back to work. Here comes the boss."

High in her Gallywood tower, Betty Neezquaff cracked her knuckles and smiled. All was proceeding as she had foreseen…

CHAPTER 13

I have wondered, at times, if God employs secret agents behind enemy lines. Perhaps in the deepest circles of Hell there are holy angels toiling away in disguise, collecting intelligence to send up to Heaven and, from time to time, easing the suffering of the damned while the Devil is distracted.

If so, Rufus Camford would almost certainly be one of them.

For decades, he had toiled away in the muck and filth, breathed the noisome air that poisons the soul, and moved among the worst specimens of sentient life to be found anywhere in the known universe. In short, he had lived and worked in Gallywood.

And yet, no one had a bad word to say about the man. He did people favors without expecting recompense. He never indulged in gossip or associated himself with any of the odious whisper campaigns that had brought down so many giants of the industry. No one could recall him ever attending an orgy or participating in the dark rites that bound virtually everyone in Gallywood to one another. He treated everyone with respect, from the valet parkers on the studio lot to disgraced A-listers whose careers needed mending. Most remarkably, he was even kind to writers.

Even more extraordinarily, for a Gallywood mogul, he was humble, always deflecting compliments towards his subordinates with a folksy aphorism of some kind.

As such, Betty Neezquaff hated him with the burning

heat of a thousand suns.

I do not know if Camford was even aware of this, but if he was, it certainly didn't trouble him. On the contrary, I imagine he offered silent prayers for Betty's immortal soul, which, had she known of them, would only have added fuel to the fire of her enmity.

On this particular morning, Camford was conducting a meeting with the marketing team for *Star Attack* when his assistant interrupted him.

"Mr. Camford. Sorry to interrupt, but Ms. Neezquaff is here. She says it is of the utmost importance that she speaks with you."

Sitting in the reception area, Betty Neezquaff imagined herself the living embodiment of the Death Moon, a dreadful weapon devised by the emperor, capable of wiping out entire planets in a single blast and leaving behind nothing but a floating field of debris by way of evidence.

To heighten dramatic tension, the *Star Attack* movies always showed the Death Moon slowly maneuvering into position so that it could get a clear line of fire on the unsuspecting planet it was about to destroy. This also had the benefit of giving the good guys a window of opportunity in which to come up with a last-ditch plan, which almost always involved blowing up the Death Moon in the nick of time. This annoyed the emperor greatly, and he usually responded by building yet another, even larger, Death Moon for the next installment.

At any rate, this was not the day to fire the main weapon. This was a day for moving into position.

The marketing shmoes smiled nervously as they passed Neezquaff, and Camford's assistant gave her the green light to enter his office.

"Ah, Betty," said the mogul, as courteous as ever, though he was not facing her. "Always a pleasure to see you! Can I offer you any refreshments?"

"No, Mr. Camford," she replied sternly. "I only need a

moment of your valuable time."

He beckoned for her to sit.

"First of all," she began, "let me say what a pleasure it has been to work with your talented niece. Genius clearly runs in the family."

It was then that she first noticed it, something uncanny and different about the man. Something that unsettled her on a deep level, that gave her the impression of walls closing in about her with no possibility of escape.

He had grown a beard. It was short and quite well-trimmed, but there was no mistaking it. Upon his previously smooth face, was a beard!

No one at the network wore beards. The last person to do so was the founder himself. And when he had shown up one morning, after a three-day weekend, with a swathe of rakish stubble on his face, the board of directors quickly convened to usher him into early retirement.

Betty was determined not to give in to fear, not to even speak of it. And yet, at that moment, it was all she could think about.

Camford, for his part, seemed utterly nonplussed and smiled at her neutrally.

"That is most kind of you to say, Betty," he said, responding to the unanticipated praise she had heaped upon his niece. "I am inordinately proud of her."

"Yes, ahem, well…" she spluttered, struggling to regain her composure. "At any rate, I merely wanted to let you know that she has arrived safely on Rexos-4 and has taken up residence with two of the locals. We have some excellent footage that should air this evening."

"Marvelous. I shall be sure to tune in." There followed a silence. A most dreadful, smiling silence.

"Right," said Betty, eyeing the exit. "I should get back to it, then. Toodle-oo."

Once safely back in her own office, she collapsed into her chair and patted her perfectly coiffed hair. A beard? Has he gone mad? What could it mean?

As if on cue, her private line rang, the one that only sounded on official mafia business

Trembling, she answered it.

The voice on the other end was a model of decorous civility. "Ms. Neezquaff," it said. "It has been too long since we last spoke. How are you faring?"

She cleared her throat. "Mr. Kratsch. I do hope everything is well. I...I am doing as you instructed."

"Are you?" said the boss. "Well, that is a relief. I was becoming concerned that perhaps you were freelancing a bit on this latest assignment."

The implication was dire. If there's one thing you can't get away with in any mafia, it's freelancing.

"No! Absolutely not, sir! I wouldn't dream of it."

"Good. Then I trust that your plan to subvert the ending of *What's the Bloody Point?* is proceeding as planned?"

"Yes, sir. Ratings have been through the roof since we announced the lottery — and I expect they'll continue to climb until the final episode when we will of course announce that the rescue mission has failed…"

The silence on the line unnerved her, and she felt obliged to fill it with more words.

"…I, er, did take it upon myself to send Camford's niece to the planet. I expect that when she is killed along with the rest of the cast, it will spell the end for our little fly in the ointment."

Suddenly, what had seemed to her an inspired bit of opportunistic improvisation now appeared fraught with danger.

"This, I noticed," said Kratsch without emotion. "Do you really think it wise to involve her in our affairs? She is a civilian after all."

"With respect, sir, she is hardly a civilian. She's Camford's most treasured niece, and besides, she's in the business now."

"And how did old Rufus react to this?"

Well, if Betty was nervous before, this question very nearly sent her into apoplexy.

"Actually, he hasn't really reacted much at all," she ventured. "I don't think he suspects a thing, although..."

"Go on," said Kratsch.

"Although when I met with him, just now, he -- he had grown a beard."

Do you suppose that the pits of Hell are filled with the sounds of wailing and moaning and the gnashing of teeth? They are not. Such things would be a veritable comfort to those damned to be there. No, Hell is quite silent, for there is nothing more terrifying than silence, as Betty Neezquaff was now discovering.

After what seemed an eternity, Kratsch finally spoke. "A beard, eh?" Then he laughed, and not in a friendly, reassuring way, let me assure you. It was one of those knowing sort of laughs that you hear from villains in the old classic horror movies.

His villainous laugh stopped abruptly. "That can mean only two things."

"What are those?" gulped Betty.

"Well, the common reason for a man growing a beard is that he has something to hide. It's a psychological defense mechanism that spans nearly all species. A beard is like a shield, Ms. Neezquaff. A shield against the unwanted gaze of the outside world."

"And what is the second explanation?"

"An abundance of confidence," said Kratsch, his voice now a pugnacious rasp, "A sign that was intended for you, and therefore for me. For the head of the studio to grow a beard, he must either be insane or supremely confident in his position. Say what you will about Rufus Chapek, but he is far from insane. He is our most formidable adversary, Neezquaff. Underestimate him at your peril. I fear he may already be a few steps ahead you."

It shocked Betty to hear the head of her order speak in such terms of the man she considered to be a bit of a buffoon.

"I assure you, Mr. Kratsch, I am well out in front."

"For your sake, I hope that is true. Still, I think you would be wise to put your most competent person on the case. Yes, you should find that person and send them to Rexos-4 with immediate effect, to be your eyes and ears on the ground. Am I quite clear?"

"Absolutely!"

"Good day to you, then. I shall be monitoring your progress with great interest." And with that, the call ended.

You may think that Betty was relieved. And I suppose she was in some respects. One never knew how a call with Kratsch might end, but still being alive and employed by the end of one could be counted as a small victory.

On the other hand, she was now fixedly under the scrutiny of the most terrifying man in the known universe, and she had to deliver the goods. Worse, she didn't really know of anyone with any appreciable competence. This is one of the downsides regarding mafias, you see. Amidst all the turf-protecting, rival-killing, and the tying-on of figurative cement shoes, it's dashed hard to retain high quality talent. The coin of the realm was bullying, and she had access to that in abundance. But in this instance, it was rather like having a pocket full of pennies at a vending machine.

And so she sat there for several minutes, fretting frightfully, until it dawned on her that the answer was waiting right outside her door, so to speak. She did know one exceptionally competent person after all.

"Edwina!" she shouted. "Come in here at once. I have an assignment for you."

CHAPTER 14

"I think it's perhaps best," said Gumpilos to Elvie Renfro, "that we don't clue everyone in on your presence here. The planet's going through an awful lot at the moment, and I'm not sure how they would respond to the actual physical presence of an alien, if you'll pardon the term."

Elvie concurred. Much as she wanted to get out of the house and see the sights of Rexos-4, she didn't want to cause a major diplomatic incident.

And the arrangement did have its benefits. Gumpilos was able to continue his work at the time capsule company, while Elvie proved to be a remarkably attentive and reliable babysitter for the infant Tfliximop. This allowed Cniphia the opportunity for some alone time now and then.

Ah, yes ... you've noticed the child. The desert rose! The symbol of hope and renewal! How could I forget? He was born after just eight and a half weeks, a bit early, but nothing to be alarmed about. He was named Gusto, though everyone called him Gus.

Gus's arrival was met with all the joy and delight you might imagine, a ray of sunshine in the gathering darkness so to speak. In order to keep Elvie's presence a secret, visitors were strictly limited, and by strictly limited, I mean that no one other than Gumpilos's parents were allowed to come by the house. This suited the couple just fine, for marriage had not so much transformed them into homebodies as it had revealed homebodied-ness to be the long-held desire of their hearts.

It must also be said that there was a mild degree of scandal and social censure associated with having a baby this late in the game. Many considered it to be a cruelty, and really rather selfish of them. Whenever Cniphia took Gus to the grocery store or the park, she was inevitably greeted with disapproving looks and barely concealed whispers. This irritated Gumpilos in the extreme, but he held his tongue at his wife's request.

Elvie, on the other hand, was absolutely smitten with the baby. Perhaps it had stirred a latent maternal instinct in her, or perhaps she just enjoyed having someone very nearly her own size around. Who can say? For his part, baby Gus was rather dubious about this odd-looking creature. The ethics of early exposure to other sentient life forms had been a hotly-debated topic in recent years. Traditionalists maintained that it risks interfering with a child's still-developing sense of self, while progressives wholeheartedly recommend it as a means of warding off intolerance later in life. I say that if there is one department in which babies are not lacking, it is self-centeredness, and given that we live in a vast galaxy, one might as well take a gander at the vast and beautiful diversity of life it contains. On the question of the Croakilids, however, there is universal agreement. Not only are they widely regarded as the rudest species in the known universe, but they also have an unwholesome tendency to eat other people's children.

Elvie, as we have noted, was like an onion, only her layers revealed nothing but steadfast kindness all the way to the core, and so she steadfastly enchanted Gus with funny faces and tickles despite his natural skepticism.

Still, being cooped up in a house around the clock, even a house as full of warmth and conviviality as the Tfliximops' residence, does have the tendency to wear one down, and Elvie was beginning to succumb to the effects of cabin fever. This did not go unnoticed by her hosts, who, on a particularly purpurescent Saturday afternoon, came up with a rather splendid idea.

"Elvie," said Cniphia. "We were thinking of taking Gus out in the pram to see some sights. Would you like to come along?"

This development was puzzling for Elvie.

First, nothing had changed in their circumstances to warrant risking the sudden exposure of Elvie's presence on Rexos-4. Two parents walking about the neighborhood with a newborn and a tiny alien in tow was bound to attract unwanted attention.

Second, Elvie, as much as she would have liked to get some fresh air, was far more interested in the grand natural wonders of Rexos-4 that she had seen on the show over the years. The Tfliximops' neighborhood was quite safe and lovely and full of good schools and the like, but it was, in the end, a rather dull suburb.

As is so often the case in such situations, this confusion happened as the result of differences in language. You see, in most places around the galaxy, a pram is a frilly little contraption with wheels and a sunshade, and perhaps a holder next to the handles for mom or dad to store a cup of coffee as they push junior around on leafy sidewalks.

On Rexos-4, a pram is something altogether different.

Sensing Elvie's perplexity, Gumpilos beckoned her to the garage. Cniphia followed on, bouncing baby Gus in her arms.

"Now where did I store the deuced thing?" muttered Gumpilos as he rummaged about in a storage locker tucked away behind his car. "Aha! Here it is!"

Amidst a clutter of garden tools, brooms, and other implements, Gumpilos hoisted a box that apparently contained the very object he had been seeking. He carried it back inside the house, and opened it.

"Right," he said. "Let's just have a squiz at the assembly manual."

Now, if you happen to know any fathers, or are perhaps a father yourself, you may anticipate what happened next, for assembly manuals are known throughout the galaxy to be the most indecipherable documents in existence.

In less civilized times, they were even used as torture devices, until the Convention of 270,245 outlawed them in favor of more humane methods: such as the rack; the pear of anguish; drawing and quartering, and the like. They are designed not so much to assist in the piecing together of complicated instruments as to convey a general sense of hopelessness and despair and singular block-headedness. As you might expect, assembly manuals on Rexos-4 were particularly gruesome and many would rather face the apocalypse than the document that Gumpilos held in his hands.

He had the look, therefore, of a man who had just been sentenced to have a forest of bamboo shoved under his fingernails, until he was saved by his wife.

"Dear, don't you remember? We bought the self-assembly package. All you have to do is push the button. I don't think even you could bodge this up."

Because we live in a fallen world, the assembly button itself also required some assembly, but Gumpilos soldiered through it with sheer bloody-mindedness until at last the button was ready to push.

He did so.

And before Elvie's eyes, the various bits and bobs inside the box began to maneuver themselves into position with surgical precision. Within a matter of minutes, she was looking at a sleek, smoked glass vehicle of some kind, with rounded surfaces of aerodynamic perfection. On the back of it was a handle, a platform, and a holster for two cups of coffee.

"This is the Badger!" exclaimed Gumpilos. "A proper Rexan pram. Elvie Renfro and Gus can snuggle up inside, whilst we lead the grand tour!"

He looked over at Elvie, who by now had fathomed out the plan and was clapping along with Gus.

"What?" said Cniphia to their guest. "You didn't think we'd be taking shanks' pony did you?"

Of course, all subsequently realized that Gumpilos had

assembled the thing indoors and had no way of getting it where it needed to be, namely outdoors. Cniphia had not purchased the self-disassembly option, so after a few hours of whingeing and chuntering, Gumpilos had it back in pieces, which were carefully placed in the back yard and re-assembled with the press of a button.

After tucking Elvie and Gus inside the glass compartment, Gumpilos and Cniphia stepped onto the rear platform, deposited their coffee thermoses into the holsters, and fired up the pram.

"Off we go!" said Gumpilos. "Are you two ready to see some sights?"

"Absolutely," replied Elvie over an intercom.

"Mmansdefl bliexripan," gurgled Gus, though it meant nothing in Rexan or any other language. Instead, it was the sort of unintelligent nonsense that babies blurt out whilst trying to figure out how to move their tongues properly.

The pram floated into the sky, and in a flash they were off.

High above the planet they soared, and before long the great city on the bay was well behind them. The lush wilderland of Rexos-4 stretched out below, beguiling Elvie with its beauty and diversity. She saw iridescent forest canopies that sang softly in the breeze, sparkling rivers that toppled off mountains in great falls, rolling plains filled with tall grass that rippled and undulated like poetry in sign language. At one point, a flock of knupalong birds approached and danced around the pram like aerial porpoises, their sinuous tail streamers gleaming in the sun's rays.

Magical. It was truly and utterly magical, and by the time they had to return home, Elvie was more in love with the planet than she had ever dreamed possible.

I cannot say precisely what it is that makes one fall in love with a particular planet. I myself have visited hundreds of them, and they are all beautiful in their way. They are also similar. Nearly all have mountains and rivers, oceans, prairies, forests and whatnot. And yet it is undeniable that nearly all of us, at some point in our lives, will develop a special attachment to a certain place, a relationship that sets it above all other places we have visited or may visit in the future. Some will say that it is the people who make a place, and I suppose that's true to some extent. But again, people are much the same everywhere you go. You'll find all sorts of coves, ranging from the most dastardly to the downright saintly on just about any rock orbiting any given star. And besides, there are those who love places that are utterly solitary and claim to love them for that very reason.

No, I think it is something internal, as it were, the *feelings* that we attach to places. It's rather like that whole observer-observed business that physicists prattle on about. Some sort of wave function collapses, and the place and the person become one and the same.

And to think - all of it is temporary! Not just on Rexos-4, but every forest, every stream, every lonely beach on every planet in the universe. Whether by the action of climate change, or plate tectonics, or erosion, or rogue stars, or entropy itself, they will all cease to be. Stepping back a bit, one can indeed see how eternity might fall in love with the works of time. The poets are on to something there, I'll grant you. Pathos and beauty are quite the intoxicating cocktail.

These sorts of rummy thoughts were racing through Elvie's mind as the pram hovered over 1426 Ickleberry Way and began to descend softly towards the hedge-encircled back yard. Gus had fallen asleep and was cooing softly next to her, and she was glad for it since it meant he didn't have to see her cry.

As the craft neared touchdown, Elvie noticed something quite surprising - another space egg capsule had landed in the very same back yard! A touch of the old foreboding shivered her spine. It had to be someone from the network, though in truth it didn't matter much who it was. The fact that someone else had arrived on Rexos-4 was a reminder that her brief and happy interlude with the Tfliximops could not last forever.

When they reached the ground, the pram opened up and Elvie poked her head in an attempt to catch sight of the new arrival. But there was no one to be seen. Gumpilos and Cniphia exchanged a worried look and were about to disembark from their perch at the rear of the vehicle when suddenly, and without warning, a creature shimmered into existence before them. Not a hologram, mind you, but an actual flesh-and-blood being. It was quite startling for the Tfliximposes, especially as they weren't accustomed to being around people who could teleport small distances.

"Edwina Mumford at your service," said the creature, opening her arms in a theatrical fashion. "Things are about to get a bit dicey 'round here, but don't worry - I have come to help."

Elvie blinked in astonishment to see Neezquaff's dowdy-yet-hyper-efficient assistant before her. She was comforted, more deeply than we shall ever know, that Gusto, having apparently resolved to look upon her favorably, had grasped her hand and was squeezing it tightly.

CHAPTER 15

To describe Edwina Mumford as competent is rather like describing a blue giant hypernova as bright. Yes, it gets the meaning across well enough, but fails spectacularly when it comes to conveying an all-important sense of magnitude. A star is bright. A supernova is spectacularly bright, brighter than the whole of a galaxy. A hypernova? Let's just say that if one of those goes off anywhere near your planet, your blind cavefish will suddenly find themselves at the top of the evolutionary ladder.

So it should come as no surprise at all that she quickly took command of the situation at 1426 Ickleberry Way.

"Inside, the lot of you," she commanded. Even baby Gus, who understood not a word that anyone said, took her meaning and meekly folded himself into his mother's arms.

The rummy thing about chaps like Edwina Mumford is that they make you feel about as small as a quintz fly, but without the offsetting benefits of a high IQ. I've been counseled that it helps to imagine them in their undergarments, but I cannot in good conscience say that this stratagem works. If anything, it would be rather worse to be bossed around by a hyper-competent generalissimo wearing nothing but her knickers.

Once the crew was assembled inside the house, Edwina surveyed them the way a dry cleaner might look at a mustard stain on a pair of white trousers.

"I am here, officially, to oversee the conclusion of the

lottery," she announced. "And to ensure that the rescue mission goes off without a hitch."

Everyone nodded, for this seemed perfectly reasonable under the circumstances.

"Unofficially, however, I have another task … which is to save you lot. I expect this will prove rather more difficult."

Now you might think that this galvanizing news would be greeted with a bit of excitement, perhaps something along the lines of eager murmuring or even a spontaneous "whoop." But I remind you that Rexan society had for more than ten millennia lived under the doom of the impending apocalypse. The end of all life was as natural to them as the tides. Indeed it was part of the wallpaper of their existence. One might take note of it from time to time and think *Oh, that's a bit dreary, I should probably get around to doing something about it someday*, before moving on to more important matters like what to have for dinner or how to stop the neighbor's dog from barking at all hours. But as a general rule, it was simply accepted as a given.

Gumpilos, we have said, was atypical in his optimism, a disposition which unceasingly threatened to burst the strained buttons of his decorum.

"Well, I say! The lottery is coming up after all," he enthused. "Perhaps we will be selected in it? It's certainly worth hoping for, anyway."

"Mr. Tfliximop," intoned Edwina. "Where I am from, we have a saying: 'Hope is not a strategy.' The odds of any individual Rexan being selected are roughly 50,000 to one. The odds that you will both be chosen are therefore in the order of two-and-a-half billion to one."

Gumpilos blinked at her, grateful on the one hand that she'd done the math for him, but still unconvinced.

"Actually," said Cniphia who, as we have stated, possessed a mind built to rise to such occasions. "The odds, I think you'll find, are more along the lines of 125 trillion to one. You forgot about Gus."

"I have forgotten nothing, Mrs. Tfliximop, I assure you,"

said Edwina. "The fact of the matter is that the baby isn't even in the running. He's missed the registration cutoff."

It has been said before, in a blockbuster film, if I am not mistaken, that life finds a way, and this aphorism is perfectly true. Life, in virtually all of its guises, seems to want more than anything to live.

The peculiar thing is how this drive can take so many different forms. There is the standard "Rage, rage against the dying of the light!" attitude, wherein one dedicates all of one's energy towards mere survival. This is commonly seen when one is faced with a terminal illness or perhaps the presence of a hungry burr-shark.

Then there is the cockroachian strategy of simply being so low on the totem-pole, as it were, that calamitous events pass over and around oneself, much like fog.

The geneticists and evolutionary biologists talk of something encoded in DNA, a sort of hiccup that produces a flurry of mutations and suchlike when circumstances change for the worse, thus allowing randomness - if you should choose to call it that - to produce new skills and attributes that permit a species to adapt.

But sentient life, that is another matter entirely. Sentient life, you see, has both the blessing and the curse of consciousness. That is to say, it can look up at the stars wheeling overhead and wonder, *Perhaps I'll visit them one day*, or *gosh, if I were to draw a few lines here and there, that group of lights looks an awful lot like a stegosaurus or a great hunter.* Your average amoeba, on the other hand, couldn't be bothered with such things, being entirely preoccupied with swallowing things whole and then dividing itself in two.

And with consciousness, comes a question that must be answered: *What is my purpose?* People have tried for millions of years to come up with satisfactory answers. Many, in fact, hold that there is no purpose to anything at all, that everything happens due to mere happenstance. Provide a trillion monkeys with a trillion typewriters and they might just come up with a good script for *Star Attack*, and that sort of thing.

This is called "nihilism." And it is, I suppose, a perfectly understandable response to the problem of consciousness, which, after all, was rather foisted upon us. It's not as if anyone had ever said, "Right, I'd jolly well like to be able to contemplate death, suffering, and the meaning of existence — so I'll have a bit more brainpower, please," before they were born.

Nihilism versus purpose. I think, in some respects, that this is the fundamental question. Certainly a lot of poets, philosophers and ethicists seem to think so.

Thankfully, I am none of those things, being instead a mere Gallywood journeyman who has learned a thing or two over the course of his career. But even here in tinsel-town, I think, the great divide is at play. We always have a choice to make; either to tell stories that have meaning, and therefore add a little solace to people's lives, or to play around with subversion and dashed expectations, which really amounts to nothing more than narrative nihilism.

I'll be the first to admit that nihilism can be rather seductive. After all, it is an ethos if nothing else, and it feels freeing at first, doesn't it? Shaking off the old shackles and all that. But after a while, it gets a bit tedious. Consider the Rexans. There they were, zipping along a high arc of civilizational achievement and then … Kapow! They discover, one day, that they are doomed. And how do they respond? Not by raging against the dying of the light, I can jolly well assure you! And not by trying to discover some sense of purpose, either. They just sort of gave up. And of course it's well within their right as sentient beings to do so, but I can't help but wonder if they should have chosen differently. After all, the apocalypse discovered by Galfos Tfliximop was still some 15,000 years off. And in the interim, there were all sorts of other apocalypses that might have happened that they were oblivious to! I don't mean to proselytize, but it seems to me, again, to be evidence of the divine. It is commonly said that irony belongs to the Devil and not to God, but I disagree most strenuously. How ironic, for example, that it was the discovery of the present apocalypse - which led to the creation of the show - that caused the prevention of all the various other ones over the years. "You move in mysterious ways your wonders to perform!" Etcetera, etcetera.

Anyway, here we are discussing this notion that life finds a way, and my point is that one of the commonest examples of life finding a way has to do with parents, specifically the way they look after their offspring. I myself am a confirmed bachelor and have never married or had children. However, I have seen this play out many times among my more conventional acquaintances. When a child is born, suddenly the whole game changes. The most self-absorbed johnnies will reorder their lives to facilitate the protection and welfare of these tiny, wrinkly creatures that have parachuted into their existence. Inveterate cowards will think nothing of throwing themselves in front of a hail of bullets or facing down abominable monsters to protect their fledglings. They have a purpose, you see. Something larger than themselves - figuratively speaking of course.

So it was in the Tfliximop household. The news that Gus had no chance of surviving the apocalypse without outside intervention struck Gumpilos, Cniphia, and Elvie like the proverbial bolt of lightning. Rather clarifying, I should say, and rather motivational.

Elvie was the first to speak.

"So, do you have a plan, Ms Mumford?"

Edwina arched a brow. "Of course I have a plan. But I'm afraid secrecy is the order of the day. I shall inform you of it in due course. At present, however, I need to make contact with your government. I believe the customary expression is, 'Take me to your leader.'"

"Of course!" said Gumpilos. I can give you a ride to the Chancellery straight away."

"No need to stop at the door, my dear man. Just get me close, and I'll take it from there."

CHAPTER 16

To Betty Neezquaff's mind, the latest episode's ending was sheer perfection; and the closing scene where the Tfliximop's nosy, anarchistic neighbor peeked out from behind his curtains as Gumpilos and Edwina drove off towards the Chancellery was the icing on the cake.

Just the right touch of foreshadowing! She ruminated. *Or perhaps it was foreboding?* She wasn't quite sure. More importantly, it was highly relatable, given that nosy neighbors are one of the great universal constants, right up there alongside the caesium hyperfine frequency, the speed of light in a vacuum, and the electromagnetic charge.

The fans certainly agreed, with the Edwina episode receiving the highest ratings in the history of the show.

The critics were much less kind, however. Consider this missive from Sphinctilius Bradshaw of the *Gallywood Reporter*:

Has Neezquaff Gone Squishy On Us?

The latest installment of the galaxy's longest-running reality program, *What's the Bloody Point?* was a grave disappointment in almost every aspect.

Beginning with the birth of the latest Tfliximop, it galloped oafishly from trope to trope, cliché to cliché without missing a beat. There was the pram jaunt across the Rexan frontier, a saccharine mix of pathos and beauty clearly designed to make us fall in love with the planet and its inhabitants all over again. This was followed, of course, by the arrival of a ghastly savior figure in the form of Edwina Mumford, who promptly informed Mr. and Mrs. Tfliximop that she would be delivering both them and their child from the planet's impending doom. No doubt, we will be subjected to all kinds of clever thinking under pressure from this living embodiment of deux-ex-machina in the coming weeks.

All of this began, of course, with the arrival of Rufus Camford's niece on the planet several episodes before, as clear a signal as any that the network planned to pursue an improbably happy ending over the far more realistic and subversive conclusion it so deserved.

Audiences may lap this sort of thing up in much the way that Jinks the cat gorged on Cniphia Tfliximop's vomit, but this critic knows a hot mess when he sees one.

And what about this business with the anarchist next door? Seems like a pure dead end, no doubt one of those little details added by junior writers, designed to make it look as if there is a grand plan in which all threads will be tied neatly together only to be forgotten in favor of economy and broad-stroke-ism.

The only mystery is why the genius that is Betty Neezquaff, whose prior track record was pristine, would go along with such tripe. It all reeks of a sell-out, I tell you. Could it be that Body Count Betty, who could always be counted on to deliver authenticity amid the grimmest storylines, is going soft?

Clearly, the final chapter will end with something appalling and insipid along the lines of '... and they lived happily ever after.' What's the bloody point, indeed? Please excuse me while I puke...

(where's a cat when you need one?).

It went on for a bit more after that, but you catch the drift. He didn't like it. Not one bit. And neither did any of the other critics, all of whom were firmly in the Kratsch mafia camp.

You may be wondering why, if the critics and Ms. Neezquaff are putatively on the same side, they would wield their pens so viciously against her. And I would answer that you clearly don't understand how Gallywood works, or indeed how war itself is conducted.

War, being endemic to all sentient species, may be thought of as an art form. A dark art, to be sure, but an art nonetheless. Much has been written on this subject, but the general nub of it boils down to this: the secret lies in confusing one's enemy so that they can't make heads or tails about one's true intent.

Let us imagine that you are a general of some kind, and that you wish to pillage a town in the enemy's territory. You don't just gather your forces, march straight up to the walls as if you are an angry customer looking for the departmental manager, and start firing catapults. What if the enemy's town is well-protected with high walls and cauldrons of boiling oil, and arrow slits and the like? All you've done is given them time to better-prepare for your attack. So you'd have no choice but to sit out in the cold, with missiles raining down on you, having made a complete mess of the most boring military operation of all - a siege. And nobody likes a siege, I can tell you.

No, what you want is a bit of trickery, some of the old sleight of hand. You want to pretend to be friendly, you see. Or perhaps you'll make a pretense of attacking the next town along. This way, you'll take your enemy unawares and be able to get on with the sacking business in a reasonable amount of time. Wheels within wheels, plans within plans. False flags. Sneak attacks. Betrayals. Hidden agendas. That's the stuff.

Betty Neezquaff had certainly not gone squishy, not this close to her primary objective which, as you know, was the stewardship of the *Star Attack* franchise. Far from it! This was all part of her clever plan of attack.

For you see, she had sent the ultra-competent Edwina Mumford to Rexos-4 not to ensure that the rescue mission succeeded, but rather to facilitate its failure! Any chump can follow a recipe or a plan. But it takes a special kind of talent to purposely screw something up. Improvisational talent, to be precise.

And so Betty Neezquaff was quite pleased with the cuffing she was taking in the trades that morning, for it meant that all was proceeding as she had foreseen.

To wit:

The audience was slowly but surely beginning to believe that the grand rescue was inevitable.

Not only that, they were becoming quite attached to Gumpilos and Cniphia, and now baby Gus (whose action figure, I might add, quickly became a great profit driver for the network).

And now they believed - against all odds - that both Gumpilos and Cniphia would be saved, along with at least 100,000 Rexans and quite possibly more.

Neezquaff reclined in her high-backed executive chair, threw back her head and cackled like a mad Gorgon, for she knew that the Rexans, along with the odious little twit, Elvie, would be consumed in the purgative fire of the rogue star that was racing its way through their solar system.

Those of us who have been around the block could see it coming miles off, of course. You see, there is this notion in storytelling - all storytelling - that if you show a gun at some point, you damn well have to use it. The metaphoric gun, in this case, was the nosy neighbor, who had been observing the strange happenings at chez

Tfliximop and was becoming increasingly exasperated.

And this explains why Betty Neezquaff was so self-satisfied with the final shot that I mentioned earlier.

It also explains why, when the private line rang once again, she grabbed the phone with the speed and dexterity of a dragonfly plucking its next meal out of midair.

"Mr. Kratsch," she said, her voice rich with assuredness. "What an unexpected pleasure to hear from you again so soon. I take it you've seen the morning trades…"

"I have," said the boss.

"Then surely you must agree that everything is proceeding better than we could have hoped."

"So it would appear," Kratsch grunted.

Betty noted the curt tone of his voice and also the abrupt silence that ensued. "…Then you are calling to congratulate me, I expect?"

Again, there was silence. An unnerving, haunting silence. Betty had begun to suspect that her patron was not actually calling to congratulate her.

Then at last, he spoke. "Yes, it would appear that you have it all in hand. And yet…"

She felt her stomach drop.

"…and yet, I remind you again not to underestimate Camford. You see, when you raise expectations to the greatest of heights, it becomes all the more crucial that they be subverted. Thoroughly."

This was 101 stuff, really; not any more insightful than "the bigger they are, the harder they fall" and other such truisms. Betty was perplexed.

"That is precisely what I plan to do, Mr. Kratsch. The rescue will fail, and the Tfliximops will perish along with everyone else on Rexos-4, Elvie Renfro included. I have sent my most competent person to see to it."

"You mean your administrative assistant, this Edwina Mumford."

"The very one."

"And you think you can trust her?"

In truth, Betty hadn't given the matter much thought. On the one hand, it was hard to find good help in Gallywood, and Edwina had proven herself to be most resourceful. On the other hand, she found her incredibly vexatious most of the time.

"Well, I think so. I mean to say, I don't trust anyone completely, of course. But if she knows what's good for her career, she'll do as I have bidden."

"I see," said Kratsch. "And you think you are the only one in Gallywood who can attend to her career?"

Betty did not like where this was going. Not at all. She had been quite explicit in her instructions to Edwina, but she was now wondering if she had miscalculated. She was about to sputter out a response when Kratsch spoke again.

"Are you familiar with the trope of the Chosen One?"

Betty shuddered. Everyone in her mafia knew of this wretched archetype, the very worst of them all. *Star Attack* had it in spades: the predictable, awful pattern of an unlikely hero (usually a child) surviving catastrophe and then wielding the full weaponry of destiny like an avenging angel. The very thought of it shook her to the core. To hear it spoken aloud was as the first footsteps of doom.

"Yes, of course. It is the antithesis to everything we stand for, the very trope that must be eradicated forever!" She added a bit of evangelical fervor here, for effect.

"Indeed it is. And so I caution you, Ms. Neezquaff, not to let anything like that happen on your watch. For you see, the Chosen One can only emerge from the very sort of circumstances you have so skillfully engineered. We want a galaxy in which such things shouldn't even enter anyone's imagination. You are playing with fire and it would not benefit you to fail us."

Well, you can imagine how this made Betty feel. Terrified is the word for it. The possibility of failure hadn't previously occurred to her. Surely, Edwina would see this thing through? But then a thought arose from the abyss of her soul. *What if she doesn't?*

There was only one thing for it. She had to go to Rexos-4 herself.

CHAPTER 17

It is surprisingly easy for an alien to insinuate her way into the government of a planet, or at least it was for Edwina Mumford.

After teleporting from Gumpilos's car into the prime minister's office, she had matters well in hand within ten minutes. Their encounter went as follows:

"I say! Who are you and how did you get past my security detail!" yelled the prime minister, leaping out of his leather chair.

"I am Edwina Mumford, an alien capable of teleporting across short distances. I have been sent by the galactic civilization to ensure both the success of the lottery and the subsequent evacuation."

"You could have at least called. This is all a bit rummy, materializing in my office without any prior warning. Perhaps I should press the red panic button under my desk drawer and summon the guards?"

"I advise against that, sir. Privacy is of the utmost importance for the conversation we are about to have."

"Is that so?"

"It is so."

"And give me one good reason why I should believe you!"

"I shall give you two. The first is that if I wanted you dead, I would have already done the deed. I am, after all, a highly-developed alien and as such am in possession of far more advanced weaponry than you or anyone else on this planet. The second, more salient reason, is that I am in fact here to help you. Not *you* in the general sense of encompassing the entire Rexan population, but you personally."

"Do continue," said the prime minister, settling back into his chair, relieved that this creature appeared to have a proficient grasp of politics.

And Mumford did continue. "As you know, we have been monitoring the situation here for quite some time. As such, we know, for example, about the mistress you keep ... Ah, now there is no need to protest, good sir. For this is not my first rodeo, so to speak."

The prime minister's mouth opened and shut, much like that of a goldfish, but not one word left his lips. And, while he almost slid from his chair, Edwina continued to speak. "Of course, it's a common enough practice among prime ministers throughout the galaxy. And besides, I have worked in the entertainment industry. So I judge you not."

At this point, Edwina had him. But being as thorough as she was competent, she pressed home her advantage.

"We also know about the secret bank accounts you hold," she lectured, pacing the room as she did so. "The ones into which various bribes are deposited." Here, she stopped to loom over his desk and look him directly in the eye. "Again, I am not here to condemn. What I propose is that you keep both the mistress and the bank accounts, in addition to your life. And I can see to it that you, and those whom you hold dear, are successfully whisked off this God-forsaken rock and that your assets are transferred into private accounts at some of the galaxy's most reputable financial institutions. How does that sound?"

"It sounds brilliant," said the prime minister, his mood brightening. "But I say, what is the catch? There's always a catch." The prime minister, being a seasoned politician, had asked the right question.

"The only catch, prime minister, is that I shall, for the remainder of this planet's existence, rule it from the shadows. I shall be your *eminence grise*, so to speak — It seems a good bargain for you, on the whole."

Indeed it was. For the prime minister, like most prime ministers, had very little interest in the actual business of governing, least of all the business of governing a planet that was set to be destroyed in the very near future.

"It has been a pleasure doing business with you, sir," said Edwina as she made ready to teleport back to Gumpilos's car.

"But wait!" said the prime minister. "I mean, don't you have instructions of some kind? You'll be wanting the nuclear codes and intelligence files and whatnot, I'm sure."

"That will not be necessary," replied Edwina. "The most important business on this planet from now until such time as the rogue star consumes it, is the lottery and the evacuation. I will be following up with you on the details."

"But don't you want access to the secret bunker?" the PM spluttered. "I'd always assumed that if an alien ever came to visit, that they would like to work out of the secret bunker. It's cozier than it sounds."

"Again, not necessary. I already have an HQ."

"And where is that?"

"You may find me at 1426 Ickleberry Way, Flatuston-upon-Thongford. Though I stress that secrecy is of the utmost importance, and it wouldn't do for the prime minister to show up to a leafy suburb unannounced."

And with that, she shimmered in the air for a while and teleported herself into the passenger seat of Gumpilos's waiting car.

"Good heavens!" said Elvie, almost jumping out of her skin. "That'll take some getting used to."

"By the time you get used to it, this whole affair will be at an end," said Edwina airily. "Let's head home, shall we? I'm famished."

That evening, they dined on noodles. Cniphia, who had recently decided that zza-zzas in hot sauce weren't her thing after all, instead tucked into a comforting bowl of dumplings. Gumpilos had his customary bowties in fish sauce. Elvie and

Edwina, being aliens and therefore unaccustomed to the wide variety of noodles on offer, ate spaghetti and meatballs. Gus had rehydrated blorkin milk.

I'll let you unpack the noodleology on your own, but suffice to say that everyone was true to form.

After dinner, Elvie helped Gumpilos with the dishes while Cniphia put Gus to bed. Edwina had taken up residence in the basement, which was now, effectively, the center of operations for the entire planet.

It took a bit of psyching-up, but eventually Elvie, Gumpilos, and Cniphia summoned enough courage to venture downstairs, where they found Edwina poring over Gantt charts and other paraphernalia of project management.

"Sorry to interrupt," said Gumpilos. "But we were wondering if we might have a word?"

Edwina replied without looking up from her charts and papers. "You may, though I needn't remind you of the importance of my work here. Every minute is precious."

"Right. So I suppose what we should like to know is ... what happens next? I mean, the government is running the lottery..."

"To all intents andl purposes, Mr. Tfliximop, I *am* the government."

"Yes, yes of course! So then you are running the lottery, the results of which we gather are to be released several days before the apocalypse."

"Precisely."

"And then what? Will the winners be swept up into great spaceships and whisked off to parts unknown? And where are these spaceships? That is to say, are they already here or merely en-route? And if they are not here, when will they arrive? We're a bit thin on the details, you see."

Edwina clenched her jaw and did her best to patient. "The winners will indeed be whisked off, as you say, to parts unknown, but these parts – I assure you – are more than adequate. As for the spaceships, they have been hired according to union regulations and are making their way towards Rexos-4 as we speak. The time of their arrival has been carefully calculated and agreed to in writing by both network management and the union reps. Too early, and we'd have to pay an exorbitant amount of overtime while they are parked. Too late and, well … I needn't tell you the consequences of that. Therefore, they are scheduled to arrive precisely one hour before the planet is set to be engulfed in flames."

"One hour?" Gumpilos gasped. "Shaving that a bit close, don't you think?"

Edwina swiveled in her seat and arched one perfect eyebrow by way of admonishment. "Mr. Tfliximop, one hour is more than sufficient. I have spent several years arranging the calendars of well-known people in the entertainment business. If there is one area in which I may be considered an expert, it is in the management of agendas. Now, do you have any further questions?"

Gumpilos, daunted by Edwina's supreme imperiousness, did not, whereas Elvie did.

"And what about us?" she asked. "Gumpilos, Cniphia, Gus, and myself? Are you going to fix the lottery so that we all have spots? That doesn't seem altogether fair…"

"Fair!" huffed Edwina. "Ms. Renfro, fair doesn't even begin to enter into the equation. You foolishly rushed off to a doomed planet - in the middle of filming, no less - apparently without giving any thought as to how you might escape. Thankfully, Ms. Neezquaff has provided for that. There will be a ship coming a few days early to take you, me, and the Tfliximop family to safety." At this juncture, a degree of unease rose in her voice. "Furthermore, I am only able to tell you this because we are in a secure location, namely the basement. The ansible relay signal doesn't work down here. We are effectively 'backstage.' Surely you can imagine the galaxy-wide consequences if this plot twist were to leak early! Nobody likes spoilers, least of all in the final season of a 10,000-year run. It would be a scandal of immeasurable proportions. Therefore, I must insist that none of you speak of this ever again. Am I understood?"

"Perfectly!" said Gumpilos, who put his arms around Elvie and Cniphia before ushering them back up the stairs.

Later that night, just as they were about to fall asleep, Gumpilos asked his wife what she thought of the whole business.

"I think," said Cniphia, "that she is hiding something."

CHAPTER 18

A word of advice to you, dear readers: never doubt a mother's intuition. Edwina was indeed hiding something. Something of the utmost importance.

In Gallywood, as in any demimonde, there are a number of unwritten rules. But the two most important are these:

1) Nobody ever went broke underestimating the intelligence of the media-consuming galactic public.

And:

2) Never, ever, under any circumstances place your full trust in an assistant, least of all one who displays so much as a trace of competency.

Betty Neezquaff had neglected the second cardinal rule.

You see, it was not by mere chance that Edwina Mumford had ended up as her admin. Very little in this universe happens by chance, and absolutely nothing in Gallywood. No, Edwina had been groomed for the role by none other than Rufus Camford, who was, in fact, her secret mentor.

And how is that for a twist! Camford, as we have discussed, was no fool. Indeed, Mr. Kratsch had been on the nose about him when he warned Betty that the old executive might be a step or two ahead. And all that business about confounding your enemies? Well, Camford was nothing less than a secret grand master of the art. I don't hold it against him. How else could a perfectly decent chap like him not only survive in

Gallywood, but rise to the very top of the industry? To work behind enemy lines requires a certain amount of discretion. One must be as a wolf among sheep, and all that.

So the situation was thus: Betty Neezquaff had sent the singularly competent Edwina Mumford to Rexos-4 for with one purpose in mind, which was to cock up the lottery and the planned evacuation, thereby subverting the extraordinarily high expectations she had created. And had this been Edwina's purpose, she could undoubtedly have accomplished it with aplomb. However, being in actuality a secret agent for Rufus Camford, she was, in fact, working to steer matters towards, if not a happy conclusion, then at least the happiest one could expect under the circumstances. And Elvie, of course, knew that her uncle was planning on sending an entire rescue fleet, more than sufficient for the whole planet, and yet was under strict orders not to mention this to anyone. Edwina, who had not been taken into the inner sanctum of Camford's plan, was unaware of this alternative ending he had planned.

It's all very Byzantine, and I shouldn't wonder if you were a bit confused by it. Gobsmacked, even.

The problem for Edwina, Elvie, Rufus and the rest of the good guys was that Kratsch, though he despised Rufus Camford with every fiber in his being, knew better than to underestimate the man. And so he had encouraged Betty Neezquaff to see to the situation herself.

I hope that you are still with me, for there are still a few twists and turns left in the old labyrinth before we're out. In the meantime, appreciate the sheer awkwardness of the situation. Here was Edwina, doing a bang-up job as a double agent and almost singlehandedly running an entire planet. But unbeknownst to her, her boss was on his way to check on her progress. Mind you, nobody does their best work with a boss's nose over their shoulder, but when the work you're doing is the precise opposite of what the boss wants, well that is awkward at best.

Things were peaceable and productive enough over the

next few days. Edwina popped in on the prime minister from time to time with instructions pertaining to both the lottery and the evacuation. Meanwhile, the planet was abuzz with excitement. The rogue star, now visible to the naked eye even in daytime, had smashed through the outer planets and was presently making a mess of the asteroid belt, slingshotting rocks and giant ice chips in all directions. It was something to behold - a break in the monotony of having just one sun, you see. The Rexans, I'm sure, would have welcomed it were it not for the dire implications pertaining to their own survival.

So distracted were they with the spectacle that they entirely failed to notice the arrival of a small, sporty spacecraft that conveyed a certain network executive.

Betty Neezquaff did not travel by egg. No respectable Gallywood executive would have, unless they were on a publicity jaunt to some famine-stricken planet with the press in tow. Her spacecraft was a lean, sleek coupé of shiny metal and sharp angles. It had all the latest features: automatic landing assist, ion cannons mounted both front and rear, and subwoofers able to trigger small earthquakes. Best of all, it was extremely fuel efficient, a fact that she advertised with numerous bumper stickers.

It was truly a peach, enough to turn heads anywhere in the galaxy, though not on Rexos-4 on account of it being cloaked.

She engaged the auto-lander and occupied herself with reapplying her lipstick while the craft teetered and wobbled its way down towards its target on the planet's surface. Any Rexans in Flatuston-upon-Thongford, who might have been looking skyward, would have seen nothing out of the ordinary as light warped around the spaceship, sheathing it in invisibility. Birds, being evolutionarily adapted for flight, couldn't exactly see the thing, but at least had the good sense to alter their flight path around the disturbance in the electromagnetic spectrum.

At last, the craft settled silently to the ground behind a hedge in the back yard of an unsuspecting suburbanite who was, at present, tending to his tomatoes. After a final mirror check, Neezquaff opened the door and engaged the folding stairs.

From the perspective of the suburbanite, it appeared that a portal had opened in midair, as if the very fabric of spacetime had been rent apart. A being darkened this portal and began to nonchalantly descend the stair, holding what appeared to be a blaster gun of some kind.

"I am Betty Neezquaff," it said when it reached the bottom. "And I do *not* come in peace."

CHAPTER 19

As a general rule, you can't swing a dead cat in a suburb without hitting an anarchist.

This surprises many people, who assume that suburbs are places of banal contentment: humdrum, monotonous provinces, fixated on such things as maintaining lawns and hedges But I assure you, beyond this façade they are among the most dangerous places in the galaxy, veritable gardens of sin and fanaticism. Hot hatreds simmer beneath the surface, ready to erupt at the slightest provocation.

In Gallywood, of course, we know all of this, not because of any special wisdom on our part, but because we know what you are watching. You can learn most of what you need to know about someone based on their tastes in media.

For example, we know that traditionalists love sword-and-sorcery epics, as well as mannerly comedies and cozy mysteries, and that egalitarians tend to go in for science fiction.

We know that habitual watchers of the news, despite the bluster, are nearly always pliable centrists who simply need to be reminded from time to time of the limits of what is acceptable to believe. The ones you need to worry about are the people who watch game shows. Nihilists, the lot of them. They revel in staring into the abyss and care not one bit that it stares also back at them. Game shows were invented for the sole purpose of identifying these people, and many of us in Gallywood consider it part of our patriotic duty to submit lists of viewers to the relevant authorities. Reality programming, of course, cuts across this fragmented psychography, bringing together people who would not agree on anything ese,

To be perfectly honest with you, I'm not sure what anarchists watch. They're often pretty brainy coves, so it's possible they read books, which is probably where they get a high percentage of their ideas. One never knows what one is going to find in a book, and it pays to be judicious in how many one reads.

Anyway, there are two reasons why Betty Neezquaff chose to set up shop at the neighbor's house. The first was its immediate proximity to Edwina, Elvie, and the others. But the second, more important, reason was because she knew that the neighbor would be a natural ally in her cause.

Anarchists and nihilists are not the same, to be sure. There are anarchists of singular purpose and nihilists who excel at making the trains run on time. But as a general rule, they get on rather well, being natural allies in much the same way as peanut butter and chocolate or accountants and serial-killers.

Both groups are pretty keen on subversion whether it be of tropes or expectations, or governments. The trouble with anarchists is that they don't organize things particularly well. Big ideas, big ambitions, yes. But it's rather difficult to put anything into practice when you can't get elected to school boards or town councils, let alone national office. Nihilists, on the other hand, are excellent organizers, though they often can't quite figure out what it is that they're organizing. But put them together, and boy, oh boy! They can ham and egg it with the best of them.

Once she had bullied the neighbor back into his house, Neezquaff holstered her blaster and adopted a politer tone.

"I'm sure you know who I am."

Betty Neezquaff opened a lot of conversations in this manner. However, in this instance, it was a perfectly reasonable thing for her to say, given that she had recently broadcast the first message Rexos-4 had ever received from an alien civilization.

The neighbor merely blinked at her, his mouth agape. You see, like many folk who don't travel much, Rexans had not yet developed the skill of distinguishing one alien from another. You may consider this terribly backwards, and possibly even racist, but I personally prefer to see the best in people. The Rexans were not meanspirited. They were merely inexperienced. A tad provincial. Products of their unfortunate circumstances.

"Well, at any rate, I know who you are, and that's more important at the moment," she continued, not willing to stand on ceremony. "You are Pnethius Bintarik, secret leader of the Rexan People's Popular Anarchist Front. And today is your lucky day. I am Betty Neezquaff, and I am going to help you overthrow the government."

Bintarik's eyes lit up on receipt of this new information. Telling an anarchist you mean to overthrow the government is rather like chumming the water with a burr-shark nearby. At a minimum, you're sure to get its attention. And if it happens to have company, you might even induce a frenzy.

Pnethius Bintarik, like most suburban anarchists, had a bit of a chip on his shoulder. You would too if you had to live in direct contravention to your ideals, in a structured, manicured enclave, subject not only to the unjust encroachment of the state but the predations of the local Homeowners Association. It was insult heaped upon injury.

He, along with his fellow anarchists, had been waiting a long time for an opportunity like this. Conditions could not have been any riper for action with the end of the world only weeks away, aliens making contact, and the lottery occupying everyone's attention. It was literally now or never as far as the anarchists were concerned. So naturally, he was especially curious.

"And just how do you plan on doing that?" he asked Neezquaff.

"By using the media, of course. Is there another way?"

"There's another bleeding alien what landed next door a

few weeks ago," said Bintarik. "They keep it in the basement."

"That would be Edwina Mumford," said Neezquaff, narrowing her eyes. "My nemesis. The one we have to stop."

"What's an Edwina Mumford?" asked Bintarik.

"A secretary," said Neezquaff. "A secretary who has gotten a bit too uppity for her own good. But don't worry - I will deal with her." If Betty had possessed a villainous moustache, she no doubt would have been twirling it as she said this.

Now, anyone who has ever led an insurrection or plotted a coup will tell you that it's one thing to be a revolutionary in principle, quite another when it comes to putting it into practice. It's a lot of bother, you see, with no guarantee of any sort of return. And I mean no disrespect to suburban anarchists around the galaxy, but this particular species of revolutionary is more susceptible than most to last-minute discouragement. I can't tell you how many glorious rebellions were thwarted at the last minute when the leaders thought to themselves, *Right, I'd love to dismantle the structurally oppressive system, but it is a lawn-mowing day after all...*

Besides this obvious problem, nobody is entirely sure what it is that anarchists want, least of all themselves. In general, it seems to be the opposite of what everyone else wants - which partially explains their lack of electoral success.

No, if you really want to see a revolution through, you have to remember that all politics is personal, which is another way of saying resentment, in some form or another, is the key. It could be on the basis of class or economics, of course. That's a classic. Possibly religion or culture or sexual preference. Or race–versus-race is always a reliable way of stoking division!

The trouble with all of these approaches was that on Rexos-4, at least, no one really cared enough to launch a revolution over them. Eventually, they would always run up against the faffish planetary ethos–Mxtlpicam' bnak ooligapn–which was antithetical to a revolution of any kind.

So it was that Bintarik hesitated just a smidge, faced with the prospect of working alongside a newly-arrived alien for an impromptu anarchistic takeover.

"Surely you're not getting cold feet now?" taunted Neezquaff.

"Course not!" protested Bintarik. "Revolutionaries don't get cold feet. Not Rexan revolutionaries, anyway, on account of all the fur."

"Good," said N. "We have big plans for you, Pnethius. I only hope you're up to the task."

CHAPTER 20

Being on location for any extended period of time leads inevitably to certain outcomes. Outcomes, which on their own, are neither good nor bad.

For example, you can be sure that when a production cast is cut off from the outside world, there will be a deepening of their investment in the characters they play. The lines between reality and show begin to blur, you see. And even the most limited actors will at times find within themselves a range and depth of expression that they didn't know they possessed.

Another thing that happens when you force cast members to interact only with each other is that relationships will either quicken or, depending on the personalities involved, explode spectacularly. It's what mathematicians call a forcing function.

Showrunners know this, of course, and are therefore judicious, even strategic, when it comes to deciding when and whether to consign talent to a prolonged shoot. It is true that certain directors have a sadistic streak and will deploy this technique simply to provoke extreme and dangerous reactions for their own amusement. But this is rare - the exception that proves the rule, you might say.

In the case of Edwina Mumford being assigned to a prolonged stay with the Tfliximops, no such ulterior motives were in play. It was a decision made out of pure necessity, or at least a perceived necessity. Rufus Camford needed his gal in charge.

Nevertheless, the outcomes or consequences, if those were the words I want, were, in retrospect, inevitable, then Edwina Mumford was going native.

Not in the sense that she had adopted the Rexan philosophy on life, of course. I mean that she was becoming quite attached to the planet and its inhabitants, her host family in particular.

Her work of running the Rexan government from the shadows was proceeding apace. The lottery logistics had been worked out, the rendezvous point with the rescue buses decided. And the prime minister was putty in her hands. All of this was entirely predictable.

The bigger challenge - that of ensuring the salvation of the Tfliximop family - was her larger concern. We have already discussed the depressing odds against both Gumpilos and Cniphia being selected, to say nothing of the near-impossibility of saving baby Gus.

As for herself and Elvie, well, that was all in hand. Rufus Camford had arranged for a small, two person craft to arrive before the apocalypse to pick up both his niece and his operative.

Now, you're probably thinking, *Well, the solution's blindingly obvious, isn't it? She's in charge of the whole planet, so why not just cheat? Why not fix the lottery so that Gumpilos and Cniphia are both selected. Problem solved!*

And you wouldn't be entirely wrong, of course. But fixing the outcome of reality programming is a venerable tradition in Gallywood. An art form, as it were. One doesn't just waltz in and rig a ring ceremony or hamstring an obstacle course contestant, or infect a singer with Gunthan throat virus on the eve before the finalé. No! One must be subtle, even cunning! Viewers expect to be deceived, but dash it they expect a bit of effort to be put into the deception. They must, at a bare minimum, be able to convince themselves that the bachelor who ought to have won had a secret addiction, or that the obviously superior athlete had allowed herself to get cocky. If a singer misses his or her notes during the final solo, it must be on account of their nerves, not a pitch distorter secretly injected behind his ear off-camera. Otherwise, what's the point of watching it in the first place?

Of course, it helps when the talent is willing to play ball, and that is where Edwina's plan hit a minor snag.

Her plan was simple and efficient. She had created alternate identities for Gumpilos and Cniphia, both of which were destined to win spots in the lottery. This was easy enough to arrange since she had access to the central tax records on Rexos-4. With their new identities, all they had to do was separate for a few weeks until the results of the lottery were announced. Elvie could stay behind and tend to baby Gus, who would fit nicely into her lap on the two-seater craft presently auto-piloting its way towards Rexos-4 to pick up Edwina. All in all, an elegant solution, with a minimum of moving pieces, I should say.

Gumpilos and Cniphia, however, did not see it this way. Such is often the case with talent.

"You mean to say that my wife and I are to be separated from each other in the weeks leading up to the destruction of our planet? And to top it all off, we are to leave our child in the care of an alien?" G protested. As you know, it is not in his nature to be gratuitously insulting, and therefore he instantly regretted this last detail. "I'm sorry, Elvie. I didn't mean anything by it. The truth is, if we had to leave Gus with anyone, it would be you. But we are his parents after all." He turned back to Edwina. "There has to be another way."

"There are any number of other ways," she explained. "But they all involve you, Cniphia and Gus being burned alive by the rogue star. You must trust me! Is not a few weeks of hardship and separation a small price to pay for your survival? You will all be reunited when this is over, and you need never be apart again."

"But what if something goes wrong?" asked Cniphia. "You're asking us to trade the certainty of being together in these last days for the possibility that we will all survive. I'm sure that seems like a good deal to you, but…"

"…but the risk that my wife and my child might perish alone is too much!" said Gumpilos.

Edwina sighed and rubbed her temples.

"What could go wrong?" she asked. "I am effectively running the entire Rexan government from your basement. You are already guaranteed to win spots in the lottery under your new identities. Gus will be fine with Elvie, and he will be leaving the planet with me, personally, a day before the evacuation. I would never do anything to jeopardize his safety, or yours, for that matter." What she did not say, but perhaps should have said, was that she had come to love the Tfliximops and that they were the closest thing she had ever experienced to a real family.

"Please," she said instead. "I am begging you."

Gumpilos and Cniphia exchanged an indecisive look. And it was at this moment that Elvie finally spoke.

"I think you should do what Edwina asks," she said. "I know it's a huge sacrifice, but it seems to me that this is the only way to make sure that your entire family gets off Rexos-4 safely. Perhaps we could set up a rendezvous point in case something does go wrong. And as for Gus, we've gotten quite close in the last few weeks and I will protect him with my life." As if on cue, Gus made a few cooing sounds and beamed happily at her.

At last, Cniphia gave her nod of approval, indicating that the matter was settled.

"If something untoward happens – anything at all – we will all meet at the seafood shack where Gumpilos and I got engaged, the one down on the waterfront."

"Take some time to say your goodbyes," said Edwina. "As much time as you need. Your new addresses and identities are already loaded into your terminals. In about a week, the lottery results will be announced, and you'll both be on the list. After that, it's a simple matter of following the instructions and showing up at the evacuation site. Elvie, Gus, and I will be waiting for you up *there*," she said, pointing skyward.

CHAPTER 21

Edwina Mumford, as we have said, was incandescently competent. But sadly, it is possible for a person to be both competent and naïve.

In order to prepare you for the final events in this story, I must take a moment to lay out some of the subtler points of how planets are truly governed, a bit of dark arcana as it were. Now, in doing this, I am violating something of a sacred code in Gallywood, an *omerta* that is shared by all the various mafias that run this town. Well, so be it! Publish and be damned, as they say! There are some things in life that are worth doing and there are stories that must be told, even if the telling of them could mean the end of one's career.

Many people are under the perfectly understandable misconception that planets are governed by governments. It certainly appears to be the case, doesn't it? I mean, you have comprehensive elections whereafter various elected people tromp off to the capital where they enact various laws and policies. Perhaps a few years down the line, you might hold yet more elections, and a different set of people will tromp off to the capital to replace those who went before. Sometimes, it even appears that these people have completely different ideas about what laws and policies ought to be implemented. You have no doubt noticed that in the leadup to nearly any election, that there is a certain amount of vociferous jawing back and forth between the participants and their supporters. People will put signs up in their yards, bumper stickers on their vehicles, and will even go so far as to provoke arguments with perfect strangers on social media over which candidate or party or policy would be best. Even family holidays might, during such times, be characterized as being somewhat strained, with visiting aunts threatening at any moment to destroy all goodwill with offensive opinions that erupt over pudding or roast beast.

I am sorry to inform you that it is all a lie. Elections, in fact, are nothing more or less than the best reality television concept ever invented.

Think about it. Do you really believe that anything important can or should be decided by something as silly as an election? Perish the thought! It is a recipe for pure anarchy and certainly no way to run a planet. No, the real power on any planet may be found not in the hallowed halls of its government but in the offices of its dominant media.

This may shock you. It may even offend you. But consider the alternative. People are, for the most part, decent enough chaps when you interact with them on a one-on-one basis. But put a whole bunch of them together, as often is the case on a planet, and terrible things can happen. Awful things. The worst sorts of things imaginable. Without media, you can get people to vote for just about anything.

Thankfully, the converse is also true. Media, you see, is necessary in order to ensure that people know what and how to think. Once you have that in hand, well, the elections - along with various policies and laws - tend to work themselves out just fine.

Edwina, while a supremely efficient operator, had never been initiated into these higher mysteries, and this was, I suppose, her downfall.

While she labored day and night in the Tfliximop's basement, occasionally popping in on the prime minister to deliver some plain-spoken instructions, Betty Neezquaff was busily pulling at the true levers of power.

Recall, if you will, how Neezquaff had bragged to Elvie

about the presence of "plants" on Rexos-4. And who do you think she was referring to? Politicians? Puh-lease! What would be the point? No, she was referring to her various contacts in the Rexan media.

Her first planted story appeared just one week before the lottery results were to be announced:

PRIME MINISTER RECEIVING PREFERENTIAL TREATMENT? AN EXCLUSIVE EXPOSÉ ON GOVERNMENT CORRUPTION

The *Rexan Daily Times* has learned that Prime Minster Dooknurtz has been guaranteed a spot among the 100,000 "lucky" winners of next week's rescue lottery.

But the scandal doesn't end there. Dooknurtz has also seen to it that his mistress will be among those evacuated as well.

Reliable sources have confirmed that the prime minister, long touted as an exemplar of family values, has for several years been having illicit liaisons with none other than Loretta L'Plonk, chief political correspondent for the Rexan Broadcasting Corporation. Ms. L'Plonk and the RBC declined several requests for comment.

There is no word yet as to whether Dooknurtz has arranged for his wife's safety as well.

Some high-ranking officials suggest that the prime minister may not even be in control of his own government.

"Ever since that alien broadcast, things have been a bit queer. One gets the distinct impression that there is a shadowy power behind the throne directing our affairs," said an unnamed member of the cabinet. "An *eminence grise*."

When confronted with these serious allegations, the prime minister told our correspondent, "This is preposterous. It's not like there is an alien in some basement somewhere telling me what to do and manipulating the affairs of our estimable planet."

The *Times* will continue to investigate this story and will add new details as they become available…

Savvy coves know not to wonder why any particular story is ever printed or even whether it is true. They know instead to ask why it should be printed *at that moment in time*.

I mean, if newspapers went about reporting faithfully on government corruption, powers-behind-the-throne, bribes, and inappropriate relationships, there would scarcely be room for any real news, would there? No, such things are only reported when it serves the interests of the media to report them, which is hardly ever the case. Besides, if they were reported with consistency, they would lose their shock-value.

Edwina read the article with consternation. *Not good*, she thought. *This is not good at all.* A visit to the prime minister was in order.

"Elvie, dear," she said. "Would you be kind enough to drive me close to the Chancellery building so I can pop in on Prime Minister Dooknurtz?"

This operation was slightly more dangerous than it sounded. Elvie, after all, was an alien, as was Edwina. As such, neither of them owned a valid driver's license. And of course, Gus would have to be stored in the baby seat for the trip. You can imagine how things might go if they were pulled over for speeding or for rolling through a stop sign.

Nevertheless, Elvie managed to perform her duties flawlessly, getting close enough to the PM's office for Edwina to teleport herself inside, holding the morning's copy of *The Times*.

"What is the meaning of this?" she demanded of

Dooknurtz, tossing the newspaper onto his desk.

"How should I know?" he replied. "I assumed that it was your doing! You're supposed to be the one in charge, aren't you?"

This was, in fact, a valid point. Everyone in the Rexan media had known about the prime minister's peccadilloes for ages and it had never been an issue before. So why now?

Edwina paused for a moment to gather her thoughts. If neither she nor the PM were responsible for the story, that could mean only one thing: they had been infiltrated.

"Did you tell anyone about our arrangement?" she asked.

"Of course not! I didn't get to be prime minister by blabbing about such things."

She believed him. It was, after all, important for prime ministers to be able to keep a whole host of grubby secrets.

"Look, I don't see that this changes anything," offered Dooknurtz. "It's just bribes, corruption, and an affair, after all. I'll host a press conference with my wife tomorrow announcing that she'll be rescued, too. I should think that will tie things up nicely."

It is an odd coincidence, is it not, that the first cardinal rule of Gallywood – that no one went broke underestimating the intelligence of the public - also applies to politics. Almost enough to make one believe that we live in a designed universe, or perhaps a simulation of some sort. Who knows - maybe somewhere in another dimension, other beings are watching all of us even now? Perhaps even *we* are nothing but a program designed for their entertainment? And perhaps they exist for the sole purpose of entertaining even higher dimensional intelligences! Turtles all the way up and down, as it were.

"That sounds like a good idea," said Edwina. "In the meantime, I'll work on trying to figure out who is responsible for the leak." And with that, she teleported herself back into the passenger seat of the Tfliximops' car, which Elvie had parked in a nearby lot.

"How'd it go?" Elvie enquired.

"Hmmph," grunted Edwina, which was in fact the perfect

soundbite for how it had gone.

I must say, in her defense, that Edwina was at a distinct disadvantage in this clandestine war with Betty Neezquaff. First, she was under the misconception that by controlling the government she could control what actually happened on the planet. Second, she was trying to accomplish something noble and seemingly impossible - and it's almost always more difficult to make something happen than it is to prevent something from happening. Third, she was "on stage," as it were. She knew that viewers around the galaxy were watching her every move, with the notable exception of those made in the Tfliximops' basement. Neezquaff, on the other hand, was still operating in the shadows. Fourth, and most importantly, she didn't even know that she was involved in a war. If she was struggling, it was only natural. I, for one, don't think less of her for it, and neither should you.

The prime minister's press conference the next day was as successful, insofar as such affairs may be considered a success. With his loyal wife by his side, he apologized to his fellow Rexans and chivalrously assured everyone that his wife would be saved along with his mistress. Moreover, he fended off any suggestions that someone other than he might be managing the planet's affairs.

But before Edwina could breathe a sigh of relief, the next salvo from Neezquaff arrived:

Are We a Joke To You?

> There appears to be more than meets the eye when it comes to our mysterious alien benefactors, according to an exclusive investigation by *The Times*.
>
> Many Rexans wondered at the curious timing of the alien civilization's appearance mere months before the destruction of our planet. And although their apparent leader, a creature called Betty Neezquaff, claimed that they were reaching out for

humanitarian purposes, *The Times* has learned that more sinister motives may be at play.

It appears that the aliens have been aware of our situation on Rexos-4 for quite some time, nearly 10,000 years to be precise. And during that time, rather than offering assistance, the inhabitants of this broad-minded galactic civilization looked upon our plight as some form of voyeuristic entertainment.

For millennia they have watched us, lurking presumably in the shadows of our society and recording everything from day-to-day banalities to major geopolitical events as part of a reality television program.

By way of proof, *The Times* has acquired recordings of these broadcasts which, despite their generally lowbrow content, have apparently become a favorite program on thousands of planets.

This of course raises several important questions:

First, how long has our government known about this?

Second, why didn't the aliens offer to help sooner, when they could have presumably saved more lives?

Third, and most ominously, can we trust their intentions now that we know they have not been honest with us?

Some are now claiming that the rogue star itself is a hoax designed to frighten Rexans into the arms of these unknown beings.

"It is time for this government to be disbanded!" said Pnethius Bintarik, leader of the Rexan People's Anarchist Front. "They have been collaborating with these aliens for who knows how long. For all we know, the so-called rescue operation could be an elaborate ruse. They could take us up on those spaceships to be eaten. Or probed. Or worse..."

Needless to say, this was an escalation. After all, it is not every day that the fourth wall is broken. And today of all days - practically the eve of the final episode of the final season of *What's the Bloody Point?*

Edwina Mumford considered these points and, despite the precariousness of her situation, smiled knowingly. There could be only one explanation.

Betty Neezquaff was behind this. She was clearly squirreled away somewhere on Rexos-4, personally overseeing the conclusion of the show.

CHAPTER 22

Not even the dark emperor of Star Attack himself could have handled it any better, thought Betty. The finalé was now just a week away, and everything was coming together exactly as she had foreseen it.

Her media campaign had worked like a charm, weakening the government to such an extent that just one more well-aimed article would bring the whole thing down. By the time the rescue buses were to arrive, Rexos-4 would be in the grip of populist anarchy and conspiratorial confusion. Even if Edwina had managed to execute the logistics amidst such chaos, the people would be so confused that they would rather face incineration by the rogue star than whatever dark horrors might be awaiting them on the rescue ships. It was so beautiful, in fact, that she almost wept. The Rexans would rather choose death over salvation, a perfectly nihilistic ending that would subvert all expectations.

"The final phase of our operation is at hand, Pnethius," she said to her host. "Have you prepared your people?"

Preparing anarchists for anything is always a bit of a challenge. They're more the spontaneous sort. Improvisational, if you will. Still, Bintarik was ready to do as Betty instructed. At his signal, the Rexan People's Anarchist Front would storm the Chancellery. What, exactly, they would do once they got there was still a bit fuzzy, but the alien seemed to think that their mere presence was all that was required. As the saying goes, half of life is just showing up.

"We are ready," he said.

"Excellent. All that remains is for us to wait for Edwina's next tête-à-tête with the Prime Minister. I expect it will happen any minute now."

She was right. Peeking through the curtains, Pnethius observed Elvie and Edwina pulling out of the Tfliximops' driveway, apparently in quite a hurry.

****

"We must find where Neezquaff is lurking and stop her," said Edwina as they rounded out of the driveway onto Ickleberry Way. "She's obviously in cahoots with the local media and if I am right, there will be another article coming out any day now. She is using the press to try to bring down the Rexan government and open the door to anarchy at the worst possible moment."

She was right. For this, as we have discussed, was the nub of Neezquaff's diabolical plan. You can count on the nihilists to use chaos, confusion, fear to their maximum advantage. What Edwina did not know was that she would be walking - or rather teleporting - straight into the trap that Neezquaff had set for her.

Around the Chancellery precincts were assembled what can only be described as an angry mob, which was itself encircled by a large contingent of the Rexan media corps. Many of the horde were holding placards. The media corps were holding cameras.

You are probably wondering why Rexans, who are generally known for their torporific fatalism, might be roused to form anything like an angry mob. Again, a bit of sociology is in order.

Recall that we earlier agreed that stories are what hold the world together, the word "world" here signifying the whole of existence and sentient society. But what happens when a society loses its sense of purpose and meaning? What happens when the old stories - the ones first etched on cave walls and shared around a fire by cavemen and the like - start to lose their hold on people? It's a bit of a chicken and egg problem when you think about it. Do people first start to lose their faith and then cease to find meaning in the stories, or is it the other way around?

I don't suppose it matters much in the final analysis. The point is, nature abhors a vacuum, you see. And so when the old important stories lose their luster, so to speak, people naturally find others to replace them.

Conspiracy theories are what happens when a society has completely lost the plot. And Rexos-4 had lost the plot a long, long time ago. People need stories to help them make sense of things, even (or perhaps especially) things that seem to make no sense at all. Conspiracy theories, then, are a sort of denatured, and somewhat impotent, form of myth.

The bothersome thing is that they so often turn out to be true, or at least true enough! I mean to say, the biggest conspiracy theory making the rounds on Rexos-4 was that aliens had infiltrated the government and the media and were secretly manipulating the affairs of the entire population. Did people, deep down, really believe this was true? Well, that's deep water, my friend. Deep water indeed. You might as well ask if people believed that the old myths were true. The remarkable thing about sentience is that you can hold several ideas in your head at once: that a thing may or may not be true or perhaps both at the same time, and that it is extremely consoling regardless. I guess we're back again to that Hilbert space of many worlds and many possibilities that physicists so love. If a thing can be imagined, then it must, by definition, be possible. Only the things we can't imagine are beyond possibility.

At any rate, the point of the above perambulation is that even on a planet in the terminal stages of cultural decline, stories have the power to rouse people to action. This was the genius, you see, in Neezquaff's scheme, using the conspiracy theories - about half of which were demonstrably true - to get people to take the very actions that would lead to their doom.

Edwina was like many of the most competent people

you'd meet in life. Give them a task, and they'll go to town with it! Ask them to devise a process, and you'll get an algorithm of surpassing beauty and efficiency. They have large brains that whip about at warp speed. But they lack what we in Gallywood call "the sense of story", that ability to sniff out hidden motivations and plot twists that comes only with intense study of the craft. This is not to be confused with common sense, which is actually just the ability to say, "Well, that doesn't make any sense at all!"

"This doesn't make any sense at all," said Elvie.

"No?" replied Edwina. "I suppose you're right. But then these articles have got people whipped into a frenzy. And the end of the world is right around the corner, so it's understandable that everyone is a bit exercised. I'll just drop in on the prime minister and see what's afoot." And with that, she vanished from the passenger seat without delay, leaving Elvie to watch the surging crowd on her own.

Gosh, she thought. *If I didn't know better, I'd say this has the look of an insurrection.*

****

Being able to teleport short distances is a great trick, and it generally comes in handy in a pinch. However, there is one downside to this form of travel. One can never be entirely sure as to what is waiting at the destination.

In this instance, what was waiting at the destination was an extremely agitated prime minister. If you've ever known any agitated prime ministers, you can perhaps picture the scene. He was pacing about his office, periodically looking out the window at the gathering rabble in much the way one might look at a hornet's nest hanging under the eaves.

"Good God, woman!" he said when Edwina materialized. "You could at least have given me some warning. It's dashed uncanny and deeply unsettling how you just shimmer into rooms like that."

"My apologies, Prime Minister. But under the circumstances, I thought it best not to announce my coming. I have figured out who is responsible for this media onslaught."

"Oh?" said the PM, and by the manner in which he said it, one could tell that such details were unlikely to hold his interest.

"Betty Neezquaff."

"Now, where have I heard that name before?"

"She is the one who transmitted the first message, the one announcing the existence of the galactic civilization and the rescue mission. She is my boss, nominally at least."

The prime minister was on the cusp of asking a sensible question along the lines of "Why would she do such a thing?" when suddenly there was a great commotion on the other side of his office door. No gunshots or laser blasts, I'm happy to say. Just the sort of commotion one hears when there is a difference of opinion as to whether or not a person or group of persons should be allowed to gain entry.

The door burst open, settling the matter in favor of the plaintiffs.

Into the prime minister's office strode none other than Pnethius Bintarik and several members of his entourage, all in high dudgeon, followed by members of the Rexan press corp holding their cameras aloft.

The prime minister acted upon reflex, saying what any and all prime ministers say in such situations.

"What is the meaning of this?"

But the bargers-in did not respond. Instead, they stood, mouths agape, staring at Edwina who, in the rush of things, had neglected to teleport out of the office.

There was a burst of flashes, as various anarchists and members of the press took documentary evidence of the fact that an alien was, in fact, running the affairs of Rexos-4.

This, Edwina realized somewhat tardily, was precisely what Betty Neezquaff had wanted to happen.

"Oh," she said. "Bugger." And then she disappeared before their very eyes.

CHAPTER 23

"Bugger," said Edwina again as she teleported back into the passenger seat of the Tfliximops' waiting car, which was now, for all intents and purposes a getaway vehicle. With the benefit of Hindsight this was not the best choice of words to be transmitted to the entire Rexan population, nor was the Tfliximops' station wagon the ideal means of absconding from the Chancellery.

"Gosh, what happened in there?" asked Elvie.

"I walked right into her trap," said Edwina. "How could I have been so foolish?"

"Well, what do we do now?"

"We need to put some distance between ourselves and this angry mob, I should think," said Edwina. "And we'll need to reach out to Gumpilos and Cniphia. I expect the government will soon be falling in a coup d'état, which throws a bit of a kink in the rescue operation."

Elvie didn't need to be told twice. She threw the vehicle into gear and sped out of the parking lot with all due haste.

"Who were all of those people?"" asked Elvie once they were in the clear. "And why were they so shirty?"

"They are, I suspect, an assortment of anarchists, populists, conspiracy theorists, and citizens who simply don't like to miss out on a spectacle," replied Edwina. "People looking for some purpose and meaning in all of this. Which makes them extremely dangerous, of course."

"But the press was there, too. And they seemed to be

egging everyone on. Uncle Rufus always said that the job of the press was to keep everyone in line, especially anarchists, populists, and conspiracy theorists."

Normally, this was true of course. A word to the wise: if ever you notice that the press on your planet is all of a sudden encouraging the sort of unruly behavior on display around the Chancellery, you may regard it in much the same way you might view the tide running out rather too quickly at the beach. A tsunami is surely coming, and it would be a capital idea to run for high ground or, if you are a burrowing species like the Krabbaceans of Oceana-IV, to start digging as quickly as you can. What I mean is to say is, that this is the moment for farewells. "So long, and thanks for all the fish," and all that.

"We need to get back to the house," said Edwina.

"Agreed. Perhaps we should turn on the radio to see if there's any information about what's happening."

No sooner had Elvie pressed the button than it became evident that their worst fears had been realized.

> "We are reporting live from the Chancellery building where the Rexan government has just been overthrown. I repeat, the government has just been overthrown.
>
> "Regrettably, it appears that the conspiracy theories that have been circulating were, in fact, quite true. Members of the press, upon entering Prime Minister Dooknurtz's office just moments ago found him conferring with an alien who, if reports are correct, disappeared shortly after being discovered. Who knows where this sinister being is now? Perhaps in some secret bunker or lair, plotting its next moves.
>
> "All that we know at present is that the PM has been taken into custody and the government is now in the hands of the one man who perceptively predicted all of this long ago, Pnethius Bintarik. A true, Rexan patriot if ever there was one.

"Mr. Bintarik is set to address the planet momentarily, and we will carry his message live…"

Edwina switched off the radio.

"We have to see this news conference," she said. "It may be our only hope of finding Betty and salvaging the rescue mission."

A few minutes later, Elvie pulled the station wagon into the driveway and Edwina teleported into the basement. By the time Elvie had arrived downstairs, a disheveled Pnethius Bintarik was already addressing the planet live on television. A picture of Edwina and the prime minister, looking like two illicit bootleggers caught red-handed in the pursuance of some nefarious activity, flashed up on the screen.

> "My dear fellow Rexans, this is a glorious day for our planet!
>
> "We have exposed corruption at the highest levels, corruption that includes consorting with aliens who have been exploiting us for millennia without our knowledge or consent. We now have reason to believe that the entire so-called evacuation is a sinister plot designed to herd innocent Rexans into the arms of the alien overlords like lambs to the slaughter.
>
> "Well, we say 'enough!' For all we know, the so-called apocalypse might itself be a hoax. After all, we've gotten on just fine the last 10,000 years or so.
>
> "As of this moment, the lottery is officially cancelled and we will face this trying time as one people, together. All for one and one for all!"

I have always held the belief that there is a fine line between a plucky musketeerish ethos and outright communism, and it rather depends on which end of the musket you're holding. Or in this case, whether you want to escape an impending apocalypse or perish in an act of mass solidarity.

Edwina looked sorely pressed, and Elvie – who, as we have said, had a mind that rose to high occasions, at last decided that it was time to take the woman into her full confidence.

"—I haven't been completely honest with you," she confessed.

"How do you mean?" said Edwina.

"Well," continued Elvie, "before I left, I talked to my uncle. I convinced him that it would be a good idea to have two possible endings shot, one that included the lottery and one with a more general rescue of the entire citizenry. He's sending enough ships that it won't matter if there is a lottery or not. Every Rexan who wants to be rescued will be able to leave."

"And when do these ships arrive?" asked Edwina.

"Per the union agreement, they're set to arrive the day of the apocalypse. Plenty of time to get everyone out of harm's way."

You might imagine that Edwina was relieved by this news. After all, it would mean the salvation of everyone on the planet. And yet she had the look of someone who was decidedly not relieved. And if the look on her face were not enough, she confirmed it by saying what she said next.

"Bugger."

This perplexed Elvie, who had fervently believed that by sharing the gospel of her uncle's deliverance she might buck up the overtaxed Edwina.

"Well, I don't think it's so bad as that," she said. "I mean, we're saved. Not just us, but everyone. I should have said something sooner, but Uncle Rufus wanted me to keep a tight lid on it."

"Yes," said Edwina with an air that one might describe as defeated sagacity. "That makes perfect sense. Your uncle has always been keen on operational security.

Never let the right hand know what the left is doing, and so on."

"But I don't understand why you aren't more excited," said Elvie. "I know I am. It's been dashed hard keeping this secret for so long. Now we can call Gumpilos and Cniphia and let them know. I do hope they won't be overly cross with me."

"My dear child," said Edwina, sounding uncannily like Uncle Rufus, "there is a problem with your analysis, one that is perfectly understandable under the circumstances. You see, the downside of operational security is that every once in a while, this sort of cock-up is bound to happen."

"Cock-up?"

"In my spare time, I have been doing some checking on Galfos Tflximop's mathematical calculations from the ancient past. They are, I confess, quite solidly done. There were no errors in them, per se. He has accurately predicted the precise date of the apocalypse."

"That sounds promising," said Elvie, though she was not feeling encouraged.

"The problem is that when the Visikoshians evaporated that black hole one-hundred and fourteen seasons ago, they necessarily had to engage in a bit of local spacetime dilation. Things began moving a bit faster than normal. Not enough for anyone to notice, of course. But over a long enough time, the effects were compounded. As a consequence, the apocalypse is, in fact, coming one day earlier than expected."

"Oh," gasped Elvie. "Bugger."

"My sentiments exactly," said Edwina.

At that very moment, the phone rang. Edwina motioned for Elvie to answer it.

"Hullo," she said. "Tflximop residence. This is the nanny speaking, how may I help you?"

It was Gumpilos. Elvie quickly put him on speaker.

"Oh thank God you picked up! Cniphia and I are on

our way home right now."

"On account of the coup d'état?" asked Elvie. "Listen, about that, I have some good news…"

"Not just the coup d'état," said Gumpilos. "But the leader of said coup d'état. I recognized him immediately! It's our neighbor, Pnethius Bintarik. He lives just over the hedge. For goodness sake, stay in the basement and keep Gus safe until we return home."

"Well," said Edwina. "Perhaps all is not lost after all! If, as I suspect, Betty Neezquaff is on the planet pulling strings, she appears to be doing so from the house next door. I am going to pay her a visit. You stay here with Gus."

CHAPTER 24

In the long and venerable history of galactic media, I don't think there has ever been an uncontroversial series finalé, that would be pleasing to both the masses and critics alike.

To some extent, this is to be expected. A beginning may be a delicate thing, but not nearly so much as an ending. How do you bring together all plots, and subplots, and seeds of plots and subplots that have been sown over the run of a show like *What's the Bloody Point?* Beginnings are a time for hope and expectation, for an explosion of possibilities. Endings are a time for resolution, for closure as it were. Beginnings don't have to worry about making sense of anything. Endings have to make sense of everything. It's a bit of a fool's errand, if you ask me. The more complex and engaging a series is, the more difficult it is to wrap everything up with a neat bow at the end. In my early years as a writer, I often thought the whole business would be better off if we simply left everything unfinished.

I see the folly in that now, of course. You can't just leave all the loose ends of a story tangled up for the audience to unravel on their own! That is a surefire recipe for anarchy, and no one, not even the most committed anarchist, wants a story that has no point. For heaven's sake, even the nihilists, though they'd be loath to admit it, wouldn't stand for that. The point of their stories is that there is no point, which of course is as sharp a point as anything else.

All of which is to say that opinions may vary as to the finalé of *What's the Bloody Point?*

As for myself, I think it one of the crowning achievements in the history of our medium. Oh, there are things I might have handled differently had I been in charge, to be sure. Nits I could have picked here and there. But on the whole, I found it to be most satisfying indeed, and I hope you will agree.

Where were we? Oh yes, Edwina and Elvie had just discovered Neezquaff's lair in the basement of Pnethius Bintarik's house. And Edwina walked through a hedge gate and directly into the neighbor's property to battle wits, mano-a-mano, with her adversary.

Neezquaff, knowing that Edwina was on her way, was waiting for her in the basement.

"It took you long enough," she sneered. "And here I thought you were supposed to be so bloody competent. At any rate, there is something I have to tell you."

"And what is that?" asked Edwina.

"You're fired. More than that, you're a dead woman walking."

"You won't get away with this!" said Edwina.

"Oh, but I already have," replied Betty, unveiling a triumphant smile. "The government is in shambles. The lottery is cancelled. The rescue mission has failed. Everyone on this planet, except for yours truly, will soon perish in a paroxysm of nuclear fusion. And it will all be televised. After 10,000 years, the galaxy will see that there is indeed no point to this show, or to anything else. All I have to do now is step back and allow my associate, Mr. Bintarik, to incite widespread anarchy."

At this, she looked to the television, which was still broadcasting the anarchist's news conference. Anarchist news conferences tended to run a bit long.

Edwina followed her enemy's gaze. Bintarik had worked himself into a lather, and was clearly building to a powerful conclusion.

"...and furthermore," he blathered, "this Edwina Mumford is not the only alien that has taken up residence on our fair planet. There could be thousands of them. Who knows? But what I can tell you for certain is that one presently lurks in my basement. It calls itself Betty Neezquaff - none other than the very being that transmitted the first message we received from the galactic civilization.

Here, Bintarak paused to allow a collective hubbub of gasps to subside. "This vile creature has been attempting to control my mind and, I suspect, may have even probed me while I was asleep." More gasps, louder this time, rang out, and Bintarak had to raise his voice above the noise. "Therefore, my first act as leader of Rexos-4 is to order the arrest of both of these interlopers, who will be tried for … well, they will be tried for something very serious, I can tell you that!"

A great cheer went up from the crowd.

This is, of course, the problem in any partnership between anarchists and nihilists. They're bound to betray each other at some point. It's simply a matter of who gets off the mark first. In fairness to both sides, the last-minute double cross is a Gallywood staple, regardless of one's personal philosophy of life.

Edwina was about to say something along the lines of, "I told you so" to Neezquaff, when she was interrupted by a rather forceful blow of a blunt object against the back of her head, after which she passed into unconsciousness.

"Stupid bloody anarchists," muttered Neezquaff shaking her head and one of her fists at the television. "And stupid bloody administrative assistants." She quickly turned off the television and used its dim reflection to apply a bit of lipstick. Stepping over Edwina's body, she chuckled, "My mission here is complete."

She was halfway up the stairs to her invisible

spacecraft when she heard a tinkling, cloying sound like a woodland fairy being tickled on its belly.

"Ms. Neezquaff!" said the sound.

She turned and there was Rufus Camford's niece, Elvie Renfro, standing at the bottom of the stair.

"You won't get away with this!" Renfro shouted.

"Ah, but I already have, you slab-faced halibut of a niece. The planet will explode with you and everyone else on it. Do you think your Uncle Rufus can save you?" Here, she affected a contemptuous baby voice and loomed over her antagonist. "I'm afwaid the wittle ship he sent to pick you up has had a wittle accident, somewhere awound Centauri Longinus. Oh, and by the way, Mr. Kratsch sends his regards. Toodle-oo."

With that, she scampered up the stairs, which folded neatly behind her and disappeared into the portal. Neezquaff had apparently decided that there was no further need for discretion, as the ship dropped its invisibility cloak and began to hum softly, the way these newer craft tend to do. Call me old-fashioned, but I prefer a conventional engine, one with a bit of rumble and smoke to it. At the very least, one never forgets that it's on and might leave it running all night in the garage.

As Neezquaff departed, the last thing Elvie saw was a bumper sticker that read, "Think Galactically, Act Globally" right next to another that read, "For a small planet, this one sure has a lot of assholes." The last word was underlined for emphasis.

She ran into the cellar to check on Edwina, who was just coming to from her recent head trauma.

"Ms. Mumford, are you alright?" she asked.

"I'll be ok," Edwina mumbled, before chuckling to herself at the absurdity of such a statement. In truth, the apocalypse was nigh, and neither she nor anybody else would be ok for much longer. "Did Neezquaff get away?" she asked, rubbing the back of her head.

"I'm afraid so. She said that our pickup ship wasn't coming, something about an accident possibly arranged by someone named Kratsch."

Edwina, forgetting her injury, bolted upright at the name. She'd heard it before, whispered in dark and hopeless places, but had never been sure if Kratsch was even real.

"Well, we can't stick around here," she insisted. "That fool Bintarik and his brownshirts will be arriving to arrest us any moment. Call Gumpilos and Cniphia and tell them to meet us at the rendezvous point."

****

Elvie and Edwina arrived at the fish shack with Gus in tow just as Gumpilos and Cniphia pulled into the parking lot.

"Oh, thank God you're all safe," said Cniphia.

"That status is temporary, I'm afraid" replied Edwina, proceeding to tell them all that had happened with Neezquaff and their dastardly neighbor.

"So … what do we do now?" asked Gumpilos, sensibly.

"At the moment, the anarchists control the government and have cancelled the lottery. The evacuation, therefore, is off." She shot a look at Elvie, one that said it would be merciful not to reveal the existence - and ultimate failure - of Rufus Camford's backup plan. It was the look of all those who are defeated by the cruelty of time. "And as for our own ride off the planet, I'm afraid that's not happening either."

"So that's it?" pressed Cniphia. "There's nothing else you can do? You can't — I don't know, teleport us to safety or something?"

Edwina shook her head despondently. "I can only teleport short distances. I'm sorry. I have failed you all."

A crestfallen silence fell over the group, and the rogue star loomed beautiful yet deathly in the sky over the bay.

"I don't mind dying here," said Elvie. "I mean, I'd rather not die anywhere, but if I have to die, Rexos-4 is as good a place as any. And I'm glad I'll be with all of you at the end. I just..." She started sobbing, and Cniphia put a motherly arm around her shoulders. "I just wish we could save Gus."

After a somber moment or two had passed, Gumpilos cleared his throat.

"Perhaps we can," he ventured. "Save Gus, that is."

"But how?" asked Edwina. "We have no way to get off the planet."

"As a matter of fact, we do. Well, not us, but Gusto."

They all looked at him, mouths agape and, truthfully, a bit aghast that he would flaunt his optimism at such a time.

"Gumpilos, dear," said Cniphia. "I love you. I love everything about you. But now is not the time for your untrammeled optimism."

"As a matter of fact, it is precisely the time for untrammeled optimism. What is the bloody point of optimism at all if you abandon it the moment things start to go poxy? What is it that the poet johnnies always say about courage? You have to feel fear in order to really display it. Well, the same holds true for hope. A man can't call himself an optimist if he doesn't stick to his guns even at the end of the pier, if you'll pardon the mixing of metaphors."

"That's all well and good, but what is your plan?" asked Edwina.

"We have to get to my office," said Gumpilos. "The time capsules we sell! Don't you see? Gus is small enough to fit inside one. They're built to last, shielded against cosmic radiation, and guaranteed for one million years. More than enough time for someone to find him. And the temporal bubble will ensure that he doesn't age at all. It will be as if he had just woke up from a nap!"

Recall what I said earlier about life finding a way, and how parents - above all other forms of life in the universe - seem particularly gifted in this area. Were I an attorney, I would rest my case at this point. But, as fate would have it, I am instead a journeyman writer and a keen observer of, if I may use that parochial term once more, the human condition. In my more mystical moods, I even subscribe to notions about destiny, the unity of being, and the collective unconscious; that psychic aquifer from which all meaningful stories - indeed all great art - must arise. And how could one witness this stroke of inspiration from Gumpilos, at the very precipice of doom, without feeling on some level that one has approached the ineffable?

At any rate, as a journeyman writer, I intend to continue until the case is not merely closed but crowned with a well-calibrated dénoûement.

"It's worth a try," said Edwina. "Quick! Everyone get in the station wagon. We don't have a lot of time."

It would perhaps make for a more colorful climax if our group of heroes had to fight their way through the typical scenes of apocalyptic chaos. You know what I mean: cars careening out of control, people shrieking and setting buildings on fire, animals escaping from a zoo and running roughshod through a metropolitan area, etcetera. But this being Rexos-4, the mood was more one of lethargy than anarchy. The ride to Gumpilos's office was therefore uneventful. Somber, yes, but uneventful nonetheless.

Once inside, Gumpilos led them to the warehouse, which was filled with rows of unsold time capsules stacked on shelves. He grabbed one, a deluxe model that was guaranteed for two million years and quickly unboxed it.

Thus do we come to the second sacred moment in this story - the first one being Gumpilos's proposal at the fish shack. And if moments such as the first one call for prayerful silence, then moments such as the second call for solemn and carefully chosen words.

"Well," said Gumpilos. "I suppose it is time to say our goodbyes." He carefully tucked little Gus into the time capsule. The child, to his credit, did not cry or shout. Instead, he smiled broadly at his parents and then at Elvie, who smiled back at him through her tears.

Cniphia spoke first.

"I love you, baby boy," she cooed, kissing him gently on the forehead just above his third eye. "I am sorry that I won't be there to watch you grow up. Life is a wonderful thing, even though it may be hard and cruel at times. Never forget that, Gusto. Be like your father, the greatest and wisest of all the Tfliximops that ever there was, and know that there is always hope. Wherever I go when this part of the journey is over, I will carry my love for you there. And I shall dream of another world where I grow old with your father and watch you become the man you are meant to be."

Edwina had stepped respectfully into the background, in the manner of a funeral celebrant, and Elvie watched as Gumpilos approached the babe. He looked like one of the great heroes of the old stories now. Kind and tall, with an ocean of feeling swirling beneath a thin stoicism carved upon his visage.

"My dear Gus," he said. "It is unlikely of course that you will remember any of this. Perhaps some impressions will remain, feelings that will comfort you in the dark times of your life that are yet to come. For everything in this universe of ours has a beginning and an end, my son. A middle, too, and the middle is so very, very important. You can fill it with so many things! May you fill yours with love, hope, and purpose.

Here, as tears rolled down his cheeks, he took a moment to arrest his emotions. "As for me, I will be waiting for you on the other side with a big smile on my face and a bowl of whatever noodles govern your fate. You have made everything worthwhile. Because you, Gusto Tfliximop, you *are* the bloody point."

And with this, he too stooped to kiss the child, whispering a private blessing in his ear as he did so.

"Well then," said Gumpilos, wet-faced and lionhearted. "There is only one more thing to do." He looked at Elvie, who by now was sobbing uncontrollably. She was not, as I may have mentioned, a great beauty even under the best of circumstances, and the crying did not improve matters. As for interior pulchritude, she had it in spades.

"Elvie," he said. "There is room for one more small person in the capsule. I want you to go with Gus."

"I can't!" she wailed. "I don't want to leave you." And it was true. There are few people in this universe as brave and loyal as Elvie Renfro. And I have no doubt she would have stayed alongside her friends and faced the purgative fire of the rogue star.

"You must," said Gumpilos. "You are the link between us and him. It is, as we now know, a big and dangerous universe out there. He will need someone to look after him, and I can think of no one better suited to the task than you. Think of this as our final request. If you truly love us - as I know you do - then you will honor it."

Elvie ran to Gumpilos and threw her arms about his legs. Cniphia joined them in the embrace, and knelt down beside Elvie.

"Take care of him, Elvie. Love him as we would have."

She nodded through the tears. "I swear it with all my heart."

And with that, she climbed into the time capsule, grasped baby Gus by the hand, and drifted into hypersleep as the lid closed softly over their heads.

CHAPTER 25

Gallywood is nothing without its clichés, and I hope by now you realize that I'm all in favor of them. Tropes, clichés - whatever you want to call them - are the very mitochondria of storytelling, the little energy factories that propel a narrative forward at the cellular level.

In the old days, or the Golden Age as I call it, you didn't have all of the gratuitous nudity and sweaty aerobics you would have on display in modern Gallywood sex scenes. No. You could tell that a couple had just finished a particularly satisfying session of lovemaking when they lit up a cigarette afterwards. The details were left to the imagination.

As Rexos-4 was pitilessly consumed by the rogue star, Betty Neezquaff lit a celebratory cigarette and took a deep and gratifying drag. Her victory thus consummated, she set the coordinates for her office back in Gallywood and engaged the warp drive, smiling wickedly as she imagined her next conversation with Mr. Kratsch. Her only regret, for the present moment, was that she would be unable to watch the finalé live, as it was set to air that very night.

That conversation with Kratsch would happen a bit sooner than she expected, for when she arrived at the office early the next morning, her private line was ringing. On a personal level, I freely confess that I detest phone conversations of almost any sort. Frustrating, I find them. Full of awkward interruptions and the strained mystery of having to rely on mere words to convey meaning. Therefore, I am always filled with a measure of dread whenever the phone rings, as it generally signifies that there is someone on the other end who wishes to speak with me.

But the worst kind of phone ringing is what Betty Neezquaff experienced that morning. The kind that somehow suggested that (a) it had been going on for quite some time, and that (b) whatever it was that she had been doing while not answering the call would pale in significance when compared to the message she was about to receive. Even if, as was true in Neezquaff's case, that what you were doing was overseeing to the destruction of an entire planet.

Therefore it was with no small amount of trepidation that N answered the line.

"Mr. Kratsch," she said hopefully. "I wasn't expecting to hear from you so soon. I assume you are pleased with the finalé."

There was again that abyssal silence, and Betty imagined for a moment that she heard the faint echoes of dark eternity within it.

"You don't know, then," said Kratsch. A statement, not a question.

"Know what? Were the ratings not what we'd hoped?"

"Oh, the ratings were the highest of any show in the history of media," said Kratsch. "I'm not sure there was a soul between the outer rim and the core who didn't see it."

"And the planet? It was destroyed?"

"Burnt to a crisp. It was quite spectacular, really. Not even *Star Attack* has showcased such a display. As I always like to say, practical effects beat CGI every time, especially when it comes to pyrotechnics."

This all sounded like good news, and yet Betty couldn't shake the feeling that she was missing some important nuance.

"And the rescue ships? They never came?"

"No. The lottery never happened, thanks to the work of your friend Pnethius Bintarik. By the time any ships arrived, all that remained of Rexos-4 was a cloud of superheated plasma."

"A success then!' she said hopefully. "So we turn our attention now to *Star Attack*. I have some ideas…"

"Not so fast, Ms. Neezquaff," said Kratsch. A familiar growl had returned to his voice. "You no doubt recall our conversation about the dangers inherent in creating such a bleak scenario, particularly one suffused with the sort of false hope you introduced into the storyline of *What's the Bloody Point?*"

She did recall, and indicated this with a meek "yes."

"Then you will also recall my caution to you during said conversation, about the importance of thoroughly subverting expectations so as to avoid the most calamitous of all outcomes: the emergence of a 'Chosen One' trope."

Neezquaff gulped. I won't say that she prayed, for she remained a devoted nihilist. But this invocation of the dreaded archetype shook her to the core. Everyone in this universe, it seems, has their own species of *bête noire*. And confronted with the beast, one cannot help but close one's eyes and murmur words of supplication. It is an insuperable biological instinct, along the lines of sneezing when looking at a bright light, or cringing whenever someone says the word "moist" out loud.

"Surely—" she began.

"Surely?" interrupted Kratsch. "Have you not learned by now that nothing is 'sure,' Ms. Neezquaff? We live in a probabilistic universe, not a deterministic one. This is the very basis of our ethos."

"But what happened?"

"After you left, it seems that Gumpilos Tfliximop had what can only be described as a moment of inspiration. He sent the youngling up in one of his company's time capsules, along with Elvie Renfro. Of course, we tried to intercept it as soon as we learned what had happened, but unfortunately, Rufus Camford's agent got to it first."

"Rufus? But who did he send?"

"Edwina Mumford. Apparently, she is an artificial intelligence, and she saved a backup of herself before venturing to Rexos-4."

"Oh," said Betty, her black heart deflating like a tired balloon. "Bugger."

"Bugger doesn't begin to cover it, Ms. Neezquaff. This is a catastrophe. Worse, it is a eucatastrophe. The entire galaxy should be wallowing in the utter meaningless of all existence, and now instead, they feel the stirrings of hope. Many now look to the child as The Chosen One, anointed by destiny itself. I'm sure I don't need to tell you how disappointed I am in you. And you were so close."

In matters of good and evil and eschatology, dear readers, "close" is a cold comfort indeed.

"Am I to be ... eliminated, then?" asked Betty. A reasonable question, considering the far-reaching consequences of her failure.

Kratsch laughed one of those frightful villainous laughs of his. "Eliminated? Oh no. That would be far too easy and far too generous. Besides, we've invested too heavily in you. No, you will need to be rehabilitated. Re-educated, as it were."

Neezquaff did not like where this was going.

"What does that mean?"

"It means that you will be spending the next few years overseeing several bottom-rung soap operas. If you demonstrate any of your former talent for subverting expectations and eliminating tropes there, then I will perhaps have use for you once again."

If this were an old Gallywood production, the camera would zoom in for a close-up, and Betty Neezquaff would scream, "Noooooo!" into the void. But we are telling a modern story here, a parable for the here-and-now, and so instead she simply said, "Yes, of course, Mr. Kratsch," and hung up the phone in a stupor.

EPILOGUE

If you've made it this far, dear reader, you are probably expecting me now to pontificate a bit. After all, that is what epilogues are for, and my editor tells me that I have a general tendency in this direction.

Well, I am sorry to disappoint you, but I intend to use this last flurry of words to describe a scene that was not depicted in the show at all, one that - on account of my status as a journeyman writer with full access to the network commissary - I was privileged to overhear personally. I believe it is of the utmost importance, for it sheds light on not only the recent events on Rexos-4 but on events to come.

However, if I were to pontificate, I would say that the final results of our story are something of a mixed bag. Yes, Elvie survived, along with baby Gus - the boy that lived. Edwina Mumford, it turns out, was an almost indestructible example of artificial intelligence, which helps explain her maximal competence as well as some of the blind spots that plagued her on Rexos-4. Live and learn, as the saying goes. Rufus Camford remained atop the network empire with as firm a grip on the mandate of Heaven as ever. Betty Neezquaff had been relegated to daytime soap operas where, presumably, the damage she might cause could be minimized. And of course, *Star Attack* was safe from the subversion mafia, at least for the time being.

On the other side of the ledger, Rexos-4, and all of its inhabitants were gone, including our beloved Gumpilos and Cniphia. And a show that had provided mostly wholesome entertainment for over ten millennia was now destined for re-runs only. Reality shows, I must tell you, don't perform particularly well in syndication.

I have noticed that life is often like this. A rummy blend of good and evil, suffering and joy, hope and despair. You never know when you're going to get a happy ending or some kind of tragedy. Very often, it is a bit of both. It is one's attitude towards what happens that seems to carry the day. This was something that Gumpilos Tfliximop, in his unostentatious wisdom knew all too well.

At any rate, I have promised my editor not to pontificate any more than is absolutely necessary, and so I will leave you with the conversation I overheard between Elvie and her uncle Rufus.

The scene was, as I said, in the company cafeteria. Elvie and her old uncle Rufus were tucked away in a corner booth, with baby Gusto in a carrier.

"What is the matter, Elvie?" asked the mogul, having finished his salad with unusual speed and vigor. "You seem down. Is it about your friends, the Tfliximops?"

At the sound of his last name, baby Gus emitted a contented belch and cooed at Elvie.

"Yes," she said. "And no."

This is the sort of answer that is bound to get an entertainment executive's attention, and so Rufus leaned in, his eyes widened and his attention squarely upon his niece.

"I mean, I miss them dearly," said Elvie. "And of course I wish we had been able to save them. But I can't help but feel as if they are somehow still with me. Not just figuratively, in the sense that I am raising their son. But…"

"Spiritually?" asked Camford.

"Yes. There are times when I can almost hear Gumpilos's voice or smell Cniphia's perfume."

Camford leaned back and stroked his now fully-grown beard. "Hmmm," he murmured. "I believe you, Elvie. And in a way, it makes sense, doesn't it? I mean, if anything in this universe might be eternal, it would almost have to be love wouldn't it? And what do you suppose existed before the universe even came into being? Something had to want to make it all happen. Something had to desire it as a good. Eternity falls in love with the works of time because time is the most beautiful work of eternity."

Elvie didn't respond to this. She was young after all, and preoccupied with thoughts of her friends and of the child for whom she was now responsible.

"I like the beard, Uncle," she said after a pause. "It makes you look rather rakish. Rather piratical, in fact. Will you keep it?"

"I haven't decided yet," replied Rufus. His eyes twinkling. "I suppose there's no harm in letting it grow out a bit. It will keep the bean counters and insurrectionists on their toes."

"What will happen to Ms. Neezquaff?" asked Elvie.

"Ah, well, I had expected her to make a bid for *Star Attack* after finishing up the show. But she told me just the other day that she'd prefer a bit of a breather. Said something about wanting to work on soap operas. I expect it will be good for her. It's dashed hard to subvert a soap, you know?"

"Back on Rexos-4, she mentioned a name I had never heard before. Something about a Mr. Kratsch?"

Camford's face grew serious.

"Ah, old Mr. Kratsch," he said, stroking his beard once again, but this time it was with a wry smile on his face. "I suspected as much, but it is good to have confirmation. Well, we needn't worry about him for now. What's that old saying? 'The devil bites his own tail.' Yes, that's the one. On a more pleasant topic, we should discuss your future. What will you do next? You have so many opportunities after your performance in *What's the Bloody Point?* I thought perhaps you might enjoy working on the next episode of *Star Attack*. The writers are insisting on doing something different, something not involving a new Death Moon. I told them…"

"Actually, Uncle, I was hoping to speak with you about that. In light of the success of *What's the Bloody Point?*, it seems a shame to let the franchise go kaput."

Camford smiled. "And what do you propose, Elvie?"

"Well, I was thinking that perhaps, after a bit of time, the story might continue."

"But how? The planet is gone. The rogue star has left no one alive."

"It left one person — Gus. People really seem to connect with him, Uncle. It's almost as if they are projecting all of their own hopes and dreams onto him. One of the trades even referred to him as "the galaxy's favorite adopted child.""

"He does have a bit of the glow of destiny about him, doesn't he? But goodness, Elvie. That's a lot of pressure to put on a child. And of course, there will be people who will do everything they can to undermine him…"

"People like Mr. Kratsch?"

"Precisely people like Mr. Kratsch. I'll tell you what, why don't you put together a pilot episode, and then we can discuss it? Who knows, perhaps this is the birth of the next ten-thousand-year hit!"

"Possibly. Though I'm not overly concerned with the ratings."

"No? Well, I hate to be the bearer of bad news but it's dashed difficult to run a network without having at least *some* concern about ratings."

"What I mean is that I would want this show to be more than just a continuation of *What's the Bloody Point*? I want to do more than just entertain people. The first show was, by definition, something of a question. Perhaps this should be the answer. Or at least *an* answer. Or at least an *attempt* at an answer. I think that this would be the best possible way to honor Gumpilos and Cniphia."

Rufus Camford beamed with unalloyed pride at his niece.

"It is ambitious, Elvie. Very ambitious. Asking the right questions is difficult enough. But attempting to answer them? You're going where angels fear to tread, my dear."

"Oh, I don't believe the angels fear to tread there, Uncle.

It's just that they don't need to. But us? We're different. We aren't born with the right answers. We aren't even born with the right questions. We have to will ourselves rather blindly into the whole business. It is, as you said, so very difficult to learn which questions to ask, and I expect the answers might be downright impossible. But what is the alternative? Surely, the answers must exist. And if they do, then I say the whole bloody point is to set off in search of them, come what may."

    Truly, I could not have said it better myself.

---

[1] Actually, quite a few poets have said this over the billions of years of the universe's existence. It turns out that there were only so many ideas that could be properly expressed in poetry, and so nearly every planet has an exact replica of every other planet's most celebrated poets

ACKNOWLEDGEMENTS

As a general rule, I advise married writers against thanking anyone but their spouses first. In the case of this book, however, justice and decency require me to start elsewhere.

I would like to thank author **Kevin Ansbro** for inspiring me to become a better writer. Intrigued by a flurry of reverential praise on Goodreads for his novels, I eagerly devoured two of them in quick succession: 'In the Shadow of Time' and 'The Fish that Climbed a Tree'.

The simple act of reading his vivid prose changed the way in which I approached my own craft. I suddenly found myself buzzing with renewed energy and playfulness. He had made writing fun again!

And that was the genesis of this book, which I began to write one month after reading 'The Fish that Climbed a Tree.' You will not find a better, more inventive writer than Kevin Ansbro working today. I promise you. If you ever have the pleasure of meeting him, you will also find that he has a heart of pure gold, despite his curmudgeonly protests.

The only other writer who has inspired this kind of over-the-top effulgence in me is the great **PG Wodehouse** who, for my money, is the best writer ever in the history of the English language.

Naturally, I went through the usual editing process. **Jon Oliver** and **Robert Grossmith** providing me with superior feedback, developmental advice, and a plenitude of corrections.

Which brings me at last to my wonderful wife, **Cheryl** — living proof that patience is a hard-won virtue. I'vee never been married to a writer, so I can only imagine how difficult it must be to put up with my getting up at odd hours of the night to jot down random thoughts; disappearing to my office for hours at a time only to emerge, utterly crestfallen, at having produced only forty-seven usable words; moreover, my habit of obsessively checking sales reports and reviews while everyone else is simply trying to watch a movie...

And that is to say nothing of subjecting unfortunate bystanders to a barrage of out-loud readings and rereadings of unfinished chapters.

These are not the qualities anyone seeks in a life partner. And yet they are the very qualities Cheryl must endure on a daily basis. For this reason — and for countless others — I am grateful, above all, to her.

ABOUT THE AUTHOR

Andrew Gillsmith

Andrew Gillsmith is a science fiction writer living in St. Louis, Missouri.

Gillsmith grew up in the Golden Age of Cyberpunk. Fittingly, his first job out of school was delivering mail for Jeff Bezos when he was still selling books via Listserv. Since then, he's worked in a number of interesting roles, including head of customer experience for the Kentucky Derby, leader of a proposed hyperloop project in the United States, head of data analysis for a healthcare company, and SVP of sales for a digital marketing agency. He currently works in publisher development in the programmatic advertising space.

He is married to Cheryl and has two young sons, a Great Dane, and a pet rat named Reggie.

BOOKS BY THIS AUTHOR

Our Lady Of The Artilects

For fans of Dan Simmons, Gene Wolfe, Neal Stephenson, A Canticle for Leibowitz and other classic metaphysical sci-fi...this near future technothriller dives deep into questions of consciousness, faith, and artificial intelligence.

World leaders are already on edge as Artilects (next generation androids) begin reporting a strange apocalyptic vision that only they can see.

But when an Artilect belonging to the wealthiest man in Africa shows up at the Basilica of Our Lady of Nigeria claiming to be possessed, the stakes are raised. The Vatican sends Fr. Gabriel Serafian, an exorcist and former neuroscientist, to investigate. Serafian quickly finds himself swept up in a conspiracy of global--and possibly supernatural--dimensions.

The timing couldn't be worse. Rome is on the verge of reconciliation with the Chinese Economic Interest Zone after a 50 year cold war, and the Chinese are particularly sensitive about the so-called Apparition.

To discover the truth and save not only humanity but the artilects themselves, Serafian enlists the aid of a tough-as-nails Imperial Praetor named Namono Mbambu.

Our Lady of the Artilects is a mind-bending supernatural

science fiction novel where The Exorcist meets Westworld, with a light dusting of Snow Crash.